Other Titles by Christine Chianti:

Short Stories

The Shocking Truth

One Night

New Kid in Town

I0564999

Novellas

Whole Once More

Novels

Desert Dreams

Fiendish Fall (Sleepy Hollow High: Book 1)

Wicked Winter (Sleepy Hollow High: Book 2)

For more information or to order copies, please visit the publisher
at **www.goldenlarkpublishing.com**

CHRISTINE CHIANTI

SLEEPY HOLLOW HIGH
BOOK 3

SAVAGE

SPRING

Golden Lark Publishing

Savage Spring

Published by Golden Lark Publishing

Copyright © 2014 by Robin DeMarco Enterprises, Inc.

Cover image © 2013 by Rora Linn Images

Excerpt from Desert Dreams © 2012 Robin DeMarco Enterprises, Inc.

The names Sonex and Aerovee are trademarks of Sonex Aircraft, LLC and are used with permission. More information about these products may be found at www.sonexaircraft.com

ISBN-13: 978-0615993720

Golden Lark Publishing

P.O. Box 1602

Lockport, New York 14095-1602

www.goldenlarkpublishing.com

CHAPTER 1:

THE THIRD TASK

Tangled in the sheets, I nearly fell out of the bed when I woke. A cursory glance out the window indicated that it was indeed morning. I was a bit startled while I tried to get my bearings. Things in my life had been a little weird for me over the past six months.

My name is Stevie Nixon, and at seventeen all I wanted was to fit in with the normal kids. But, at five feet ten, I was taller than most of the other girls, and I had the basic shape of a plank of wood meaning that I had no curves. My hair was a waist length mass of chestnut that continued to look as though I'd stuck my finger into the light socket.

But I'm an optimist, so since this was my last year of high school I thought I was going to have a senior year that I never would forget. As it turns out, I was right; it's hard to forget that you've gotten wrapped up in a two hundred year old curse where anything but success equals death.

When I found the first box in my room last September, I started to learn things about my family history, things that I really had no interest in knowing. It begins with my how-ever-many-greats grandfather, Abraham Von Brunt. He was actually a very influential man. It's arguable that he's one of the two men who have made everyone aware of my home town; Sleepy Hollow, New York.

The story begins back in 1792, when a young schoolteacher named Icabod Crane was trying to win the hand of a lovely town maiden. The problem was that Von Brunt had his eye on the same girl. Apparently Grandpa was determined to win at any cost, and devised the idea of the Headless horseman to remove the opposition.

What I found in that first thin black box in my room, caused me to go through family history and even wound up down at the county court house to look at the past records. It appears that his idea of removing the competition was to murder Crane. I'm not going to say that I agree with his methods, but seriously, it happened over two hundred years ago.

The downfall of Von Brunt, and the beginning of the curse, was started because someone witnessed him kill Crane. It turned out that Icabod's great-aunt was watching, hoping to prevent the murder, but was too late. Not only was she among Crane's few kin, she was a witch who had ties going back to Salem. In her anger, she placed a curse on the heirs of Von Brunt; the eldest heir in a prime generation would have to face three clues, solve them and perform some task that the clues indicated, or they'd die.

Lucky me; I'm the eldest heir in the eleventh generation. That alone should give you an idea of what kind of luck I always seem to have. At first, I thought that this whole thing was some elaborate joke. Then I researched my family history. There were too many unexplained deaths that occurred on either solstices or equinoxes, and always in the odd generations.

Needless to say, I'm taking the whole thing very seriously now.

Seeing the sun this morning was verification that I had completed the task for the last clue, loyalty, within the time constraint. I had completed the first two, now I had to get ready to face the third and final challenge. I looked over to my desk, and even in the early morning dawn, I could make out the thin black box that would hold the clue that would explain what needed to be done to finally, and forever, break this curse.

My white and buff cocker spaniel, Misty, stretched and plodded her way up the bed to poke at me with her nose. "Hey, Girl. We made it. This is the last one." I slid out of bed and shuffled over to the inconspicuous box and took a couple of deep breaths.

After seeing the first two clues, I knew that this was kind of like that gift from that elderly relation. Not quite sure what it was, but you most likely weren't going to like it. The first clue had to be translated from Latin, and then had to be recognized as being an acrostic poem. It seemed like a lot to go through to learn that you had to be honest with everyone in your life, including yourself.

Clue number two at first glance looked a bit easier. It was a series of what looked like hieroglyphics. In actuality, it was a single word written all in Greek letters. When I decoded this one, I was left with a word that was in a language that I'd never seen before. It was only through looking at the history of the town that I stumbled upon the idea that it was most likely in Dutch, and the solution to the second clue.

So, standing over the box this morning was nerve wracking to say the least. I figured that since this was it, the last challenge, the clue was going to be the hardest to solve and the resulting task would most likely test my endurance. "Here we go, Misty,"

I said to the dog that was still sitting on the bed watching me with her head tipped to one side.

I lifted the cover of the box, keeping my eyes nearly closed. I peeked into the box and shrieked, "Are you kidding me?"

Standing over the innocent looking box I peered down and looked at what appeared to be confetti. Upon closer inspection, I noticed that each piece was shaped differently, so this clue really was a puzzle then. "Well, that's just terrific," I snorted.

My mom, Sandy, came to the door. She is a lovely woman, petite at just five-four, slim but with generous curves. She has ash blonde hair that hangs straight and reaches to her mid back, and her eyes are a rich blue. "What's wrong, Stevie?"

Carefully, I reached into the box and grabbed a handful of the confetti, "This," I said as I poured the confetti back into the box, "is my clue."

"Oh. Well, we'll figure it out."

"That's easy for you to say, Mom. We both know how bad I am with jigsaw puzzles."

She crossed to me. "Honey, you're right. You're terrible with jigsaws, but does that mean that no one else can help you?" When I shook my head she smiled, "I on the other hand happen to love puzzles. Maybe we can work on it together." She left me to finish getting ready for school.

Knowing that doing anything useful about the clue right now was totally impracticable and otherwise impossible, I determined that I would carefully put it back in the box and not worry about it until I got home. That would give me a full six to seven hours to prepare for attempting to do a jigsaw puzzle. Who knew, maybe I'd get lucky and I'd suddenly learn how to do one while I was in Calculus class.

I placed the cover back on the box and set it into an empty desk drawer. The last thing I needed with this right now was to have the box upended and spill all of those little pieces all over the floor. And since I knew that the moment I left the house, Misty would race up the stairs and jump into the window seat to watch me leave, I knew that the odds were definitely not in my favor that the box would remain on the desk. I was better off putting it in.

Grabbing my backpack, I stuffed all of my books into it and threw in an extra sweater. It was springtime in New York, but the reality was the school's heat system didn't work the same everywhere, and some rooms were just plain colder than others.

Mom called from down stairs to let me know that breakfast was ready, so I slung my purse and backpack over my shoulder, whistled for Misty and headed down. As I neared the bottom step, the smell of fresh baked coffee cake caught my attention.

I'm not sure how mom does it all. She gets up every morning and makes breakfast, and I don't just mean like cereal or something. French toast, waffles, coffee cake, these are just some of the things that she makes every morning. Then once we leave, she makes sure that the house is straightened before she locks herself into her office on the second floor where she is a freelance writer.

When Kyle and I come in from school in the afternoon, it seems that cookies have magically appeared for us, and often times they are still hot.

I followed my nose to the kitchen, where Kyle was already sitting on one of the stools stuffing a piece of steaming pastry into his mouth. "Hey, glad to see ya, Sis," he said through a mouthful of cake.

Kyle was everything that I wasn't. He was good at sports, popular with most of his classmates and he had the looks of a young god. He shared the coloring of my mom and was tall like my dad. "Good to see you, too," I quipped.

He just smiled as he grabbed another piece of cake and kept eating. My dad came through the door and began to fill his own plate. My dad was an architect, who owned his own business. This meant that while he did have an office in Tarrytown, he also kept one here at home. Often he would work three days from here, and only go into the office for meetings. Today was one of those days where he was going in. He stood there in his dark pleated pants and had a cloth napkin tucked into his neckline in an effort to protect the white shirt and tie that he was wearing.

"Heard that this last clue is going to be fun, eh?"

I just glared at him. Mom had evidently told him of the confetti, and he knew just how much I loved puzzles like this.

"Stevie, look at it this way. It's no different than working on that plane that Poppy got you. You just find the right piece and put it into the correct place."

"Yeah," I said, "except there I have a copy of the plans which tells me the size the shape and any other pertinent data I need. This clue didn't even come with a picture!"

Keeping his mouth in a tight grin, Dad just nodded and took his cake with him as he headed down the hall to his office. I looked over at Kyle, who had been relatively quiet. "Do you have something to add?"

"Nope. Just glad that you made it through that part. This is it, right? This last clue is the last part of the quest. When you solve it, the curse is broken, forever. Right?"

I shrugged. "Actually, Kyle, I don't really know. As far as I know, the answer is yes. But, if you had asked me six months ago if I would have believed in any of this, I would have said no. Now it just is."

"You're going to be the one who breaks this, I know it, Stevie." He stood up and gave me a hug before he left the room. This left me stunned; the number of times that Kyle had voluntarily hugged me since we became teens could be counted on one hand and have fingers left over, and my mom was standing in the corner leaning against the stove with tears streaming down her face.

"Mom? What is it?"

She shook her head and crossed to me and gave me a hug. "He is so worried about you, but doesn't know exactly how to show it."

Finishing my cake in silence, I went to get my backpack. I stood there in the hall just pondering the things that had been going on in my life. The whole idea of witches and curses still seemed too far-fetched for me, but what was I going to do? I slipped my coat on and was about ready to leave when Mom came into the back hall. "I thought you might like some brownies for your lunch today, and I'd forgotten to put them in your bag."

"Uh, thanks." I took the package, and could tell that they were still warm. "Mom, what time did you get up this morning? We had coffee cake for breakfast, and these are fresh this morning too."

Tears welled up in her eyes. "Oh, Stevie. I've just been so worried about you that I didn't sleep much last night. And it's not exactly a surprise that when I'm stressed I bake. That's what I did. I made the brownies around six this morning, with the coffee cake right after. Of course, I didn't tell anyone about the kiss cookies that will be waiting this afternoon."

She knew that these were my favorites, and I could only guess that she was making them for me today, but only after she'd been able to ensure that I was still around.

Emily was waiting for me at the edge of the driveway. I was still trying to get things back on an all-around even keel with everyone. The last task had stressed every relationship that I cherished: Emily and I didn't speak for almost a week, Ian and I broke up and Chrissy and I had shouted at each other. So, I was still apprehensive about everything.

"Hey!" Emily said with a big smile. "You're looking good on this first day of spring."

"Feeling pretty good too, Emily. Had coffee cake this morning for breakfast. Got warm brownies packed in my lunch and the promise of kiss cookies waiting for me when I get home, not too bad, eh?"

"Have you got the last clue yet?"

"Yeah," I hesitated.

"Okay. This ought to be good. What does it look like this time?"

"It looks like confetti. My mom came in right after I opened it, and she said it looked like it could be a jigsaw puzzle."

"Ooh, you don't do well with jigsaws." She slapped my arm, "Don't worry, we'll get you through it."

"Thanks," I said as we made our way to the stop.

Walking up to the crowd that was around the stop had always been kind of stressful. These were supposed to be my peers, but they often times acted like I was some kind of leper, and never talked to Emily or I. Today I was even more apprehensive than normal since when I solved the last clue; several of the very popular kids in the school had ended up being escorted to the police station.

Rumors had been flying yesterday about who was going to be getting sent away and every possible combination that could be imagined of how things had happened. The reality was, that I'd basically stopped a mob from attacking my friend Chrissy, who had just openly come out as being transgendered.

It seemed that my problems stemmed from Tony Despenzo being arrested and held in the county lockup until bail was met. Right now, everyone seemed to blame me for this. But there again, it wasn't me that caused this. To begin with, the real blame lay at Tony's feet: he's the one who led several other boys to attack Chris in the boys locker room before gym class one day. It was that attack that pushed Chris to openly admit that he'd always believed that he should be Chrissy. The change had been a bit hard on every one, but most of us were working through it.

The second attack had occurred over in the cemetery just two nights before. And the only thing that I'd done was to be loyal to my friend, and stand up for her, the day after Ian and I had broken up. But Ian had come when I called to be there for Chrissy. Ian was the one who had called the police, and it was my arch-nemesis and Ian's cousin, Gabby, who had turned evidence on the rest of those that were involved.

I thought about this as we climbed on the bus that was five minutes late, again. Ian and I had ended up working together to save Chrissy, because we shared the common goal, but we really hadn't talked much since then. We both agreed that we needed to talk, but timing just hadn't worked out.

I had wondered if Gabby had turned evidence in an attempt to get a lighter sentence. From what I had pieced together it didn't seem that she had. She'd given a complete statement in the presence of her public defender and had plead guilty before the PD had gone to the DA to try to work out a deal.

As the bus chugged along Webber Avenue on the way to the school, I wondered if she really had turned a new leaf so to speak, or if it was only for show until things were fixed. It had been nice yesterday, when she came to apologize to Chrissy and then had joined us, at Chrissy's invitation, to go out for a pizza. It would be really nice if we were finally beyond the petty arguments that she and I had had since we had been in pre-K together.

CHAPTER 2:

THE NEW CLIQUE

Jolting in my seat when the bus pulled into the loop, I was brought back to the reality. With a whoosh, the door opened and the throng of students began pushing forward to exit. I sat in my seat, Emily next to me, as we waited for the main group to move on. When you weren't one of the select group, it was just easier to let everyone else go first. Coupled with how things went yesterday, and the uncertainty of the super popular kids who were now waiting for their arraignments, I wouldn't have minded if we had just decided to stay on the bus.

"Come on, Stevie," Emily said as she nudged me trying to get me to head to the door.

"I suppose we've got to, right?"

"Well seeing as Mrs. Lerch is holding classes today, I guess we need to go."

We stood and made our way to the door. I was just stepping off of the bottom step, when Mrs. Kattz released the brakes and closed the door. The door hit me, causing me to lose my balance, and the sudden surge forward of the bus dumped me unceremoniously onto the sidewalk.

Picking myself up off of the ground, I looked down at what had been clean jeans when I left home, and frowned over the large wet spot that now ran the entire length of my right leg. "Why am I here, Em?" I asked.

She was fighting back a laugh. "I don't know. Maybe your mom wouldn't let you stay home today?"

I dusted myself off as best as I could and retrieved the contents of my backpack, which had been, strewn in a five-foot fan shaped pattern from my point of impact. As I was pushing my history book back into my bag, I got the prickly sensation of being watched by someone. I turned slowly, "Hello, Gabby," I said as pleasantly as I could.

"Stevie, I thought your gymnastics routine was lame. You lacked originality as well as style. The landing was good however." She playfully nudged her best friend and sidekick Tanya and they moved on.

"You know," Emily noted, "I'd really like to knock her block off at least three times daily. Usually she waits until after the first two or three periods before she ticks me off that much, but she must have wanted to get an early start."

"Well, I guess that answers my thoughts that I had on the bus."

Watching Gabby and Tanya head off, I was annoyed at myself for even thinking that Gabby had had any kind of a change of heart. She was about as likely to do that as she as wearing two different shoes.

"She may have made a small gesture, but the tiger doesn't change its stripes," Emily said reading my expressions.

"No. But I guess I was hoping that the person that we saw yesterday was the real one."

We started walking towards the main entrance. Emily was quiet for a few seconds as if she was thinking something over. "I think you may be right, Stevie. She did seem reasonably sane when we were out. Perhaps the wild card is who she is with."

"I hadn't thought about that. But if that changes who she is why doesn't she simply change who she hangs out with?"

"She's been friends with Tanya so long, perhaps she doesn't know how to make the break. Maybe if we give her time."

The bell rang, and we took off running. Hoping that we would be able to beat the odds and make homeroom on time. It wasn't even close in my case. I was still trying to open my locker when the late bell rang. So I walked down to the attendance office to officially sign in and it gave me a place that I could call my mom and have her bring me a fresh pair of jeans.

Sitting through the next few classes wasn't too bad. In orchestra we were playing a new piece that had a pretty cool oboe solo in it and was also very upbeat. We were in the last major topic of the class in physics before we took the A.P. exams. I'd never heard of Modern Physics before, but the topic turned out to be fascinating. Gym even went smoothly; we were finishing up one unit and choosing the next, so we basically got to walk around the track for a while. Even someone with my dexterity could usually handle that without any major injuries.

By the time I was on the way to French, I was feeling okay. For the most part the students that I dealt with, in passing or in the classes, had been supportive. That made me feel quite a bit more relaxed. I'd prepared myself to deal with my fellow students placing me lower on the totem pole than normal. I'm not saying that I didn't get the occasional stare or raised fist. No they were there, it's just that there were many more people who congratulated me for my stand. If nothing else, it let me hold my head a little higher.

What happened at my locker however was something that I was not exactly prepared for. I was leaning on my locker waiting for Emily, when two of Tony Despenzo's friends decided that I should have a personal discussion with them. "You shoved your nose into business that don't concern you, Nixon. Now Tony got to cool his heels downtown. They're talking about him getting sent up to Attica if he don't cooperate. Now, I ask you, why should he tell them? He ain't got no reason; it's just that they're taking your word over his."

"He led the attacks on Chrissy," I said. "So, why shouldn't he pay for what he did?"

The bigger of them shook his head. When he opened his mouth, the sound that came out sounded so deep that I didn't think that it could belong to a high school student. "The simple reason is, he's popular and you ain't. It's that simple, girly." He pulled my hair so my head snapped around towards him. "Now here's how we're going solve this problem. You going to tell the Sheriff that you was mistaken and it wasn't Tony that did them things. The charges get dropped, Tony gets out and you only get beat to a pulp if you tell someone."

"I don't think that's going to work. The Sheriff had DNA evidence as well as prints that pointed him to Tony."

"Hey! Who's this DNA guy? I don't know him. You give him the message that if he don't change his story, he's going to be very sorry."

How do you reason with insane people? There was no way that I was going to try to talk to these two about the implication of DNA testing. I knew the basics, but couldn't explain it to someone who seemed to have an IQ smaller than his shoe size. The best answer I could come up with was, "I'll give him the message.

"You better," the short one said and then he pushed me face first into the bank of lockers. I could taste the blood in my mouth as I watched them walk away.

Blood was still trickling down my face when I reached the classroom. The minute that I entered the room, I could feel every eye upon me as they all stared at me. It was only a few seconds before the taunts began to fly. "What happened, Nixon, you get a bit too fresh with my cousin and he give you a what for?" Gabby asked in a voice that was more snotty than usual.

Instead of answering her, I turned and walked back out of the room. Emily chased after me, "Stevie! Wait up!" She ran to catch up and when she did, she saw my face. "What happened?"

"Two of Dispenzo's goons tried to convince me that what I saw and know were wrong. It got a little physical."

"I can see that," she said as she led me to the nurse's office to get my face tended to. "I'm sorry that Gabby said something about you and Ian. I know that that is currently a touchy situation, although I'm going to level with you. I wish the two of you would just talk and get things resolved so we can get back to normal around here.

"Me too," I whimpered as the nurse put something on the cuts on my lip and nose.

Thoughts of Ian flooded my mind while I sat in Mrs. Murphy's office waiting for my swollen lip to go down a bit. I'd washed the blood off of my face, and now I just looked sad. I missed Ian; a lot. Since that day in my shop when I watched him walk away without so much as a backwards glance towards me, I hadn't felt whole. There was a part of me that I'd only recently discovered that was now missing.

I held the ice pack to my lip, lay back on the table and closed my eyes. Maybe I'd fall asleep and Mrs. Murphy would let me sleep for the rest of the afternoon. But that dream was shattered ten minutes later.

"Okay, Miss Nixon, I think you're probably ready to go back to class," she said taking the ice pack and handing me a pass.

"Thanks," I mumbled through my now fat lip. I headed out the door and down the hall when I saw two figures at the other end of the hall. "Ah, great," I muttered under my breath. "It's

Tweedle-Dee and Tweedle-Dum." I hoped that Gabby and Tanya would just go to wherever they were off to and not see me. Of course, with the day that I was having not only did they see me, they headed towards me.

"Hey look, Gabby. It's Nixon and she's had her face redone."

"Doesn't look like it made her look any better. Maybe that's why Ian walked away from her."

I bit my tongue. I would not respond and sink to her level. In my mind I started counting to one hundred.

"Well, since she didn't deny it, it must by the way it happened. Hey, don't worry Nixon, I'm going to help my dear cousin find someone who'll be better for him."

As they turned to leave, laughing, I noticed a shadow in the corner of the hall. Through my tear-streaked eyes, I saw Ian.

Suddenly my lungs couldn't get the air that I needed in. Ian had been there and had heard the whole thing, including me not being able to tell Gabby the truth. I needed an escape, and I needed it now. I couldn't control my emotions, and the tears began to fall down my cheek. I turned and walked away as fast as I could.

"Stevie!" I heard Ian called, but I ignored him. I needed to. I wasn't stable enough right now to face him. We had several things that we needed to talk about, but in order for me to be able to hold my own in those conversations, I needed to have my wits about me, and right now I didn't.

I found myself wandering about near the auditorium, which gave me an idea. Normally, I would have participated in the annual school musical by working on the stage crew. However this year, I spent too much time worrying about the curse. But that didn't change the fact that I still knew the combination to the door that would lead to the catwalks above the aud. It was a place that I could go, and very few people would think to look for me there.

Five minutes later, I was sitting in the dark thirty feet above the auditorium. I leaned against the bare walls, and closed my eyes. I needed to find a way to center myself and get control of my emotions.

I realized that I was breathing hard, and shaking. My skin had become clammy. "Wonderful," I told the darkness. "I'm up here and having a panic attack. Haven't I had enough today?"

I closed my eyes, and using the techniques that I had been taught years ago, began the process of forcing myself to calm down. By the time I had managed to actually get myself to relax, I heard the bell ring. I'd missed French entirely, and since I'd signed out of the health office but not returned to class, I'd have to answer for that. But that was a problem for tomorrow. Since I had lunch right now, no one would really care if I didn't show up.

I waited for fifteen minutes before I decided on my next move. Gabby was also in my lunch, and I just didn't really want to deal with her right now. The best answer would be for me to disappear right now and put a little distance between us.

Cautiously, I climbed down from the catwalk and looked out into the hall. Before I left the protection of my hiding place, I did something that I'd never done before; I forged a note to get me out of class for the rest of the day.

Stepping in the small attendance office, I told the secretary who was handling the desk that I'd forgotten to turn in my note that morning. She gave the note a cursory glance and wrote out my pass. Five minutes later, I was out.

I immediately headed towards the back of the building and the student lot. But this wasn't where I was headed. As soon as I was in the parking area, I angled and made my way to the woods, and the clearing that I had spent so much time in.

As soon as I entered the clearing, a feeling of peace swept over me. It was very hard for me to describe; all of the tensions that I had been feeling in the building were now gone.

I walked around the perimeter of the clearing. It was much the same as it was the first time that I'd come here, and all of the times I'd returned in my dreams. A large gray boulder, that was nearly the size of a school bus, sat in the middle of the clearing. Around the edges of the clearing, lay five small piles of stones.

When I'd first seen the clearing, I'd erroneously thought that they defined the edges of a circle. But as I walked it today, I realized that the points weren't the same distance from the center. There were points that were directly across from one another except for one point.

I can't explain why, but I knew that I needed to see the actual shape of the object that the rocks bordered.

I pulled a small pad of paper from my purse and began pacing off the distance between stones. By using some very basic estimation, I was able to make a crude sketch of the shape. I didn't see anything until I connected the dot; a pentagram.

"I should have known. If there's a witch involved, she needs a pentagram." I told the empty clearing. I walked to the center of the clearing. There was definitely something that I passed through that was about ten feet from the boulder. I couldn't really explain the feeling that I had when I passed this point, but I definitely felt it. I decided that it may end up being important, so I again used my feelings and my powers of estimation to make a simple map on the diagram of the pentagram that I had.

I stared at each pile of stones, and then walked until I had that 'feeling' like I'd just run into the edge of power. I was able to get a fairly decent idea of where this power was finally from this map.

When I looked at it, I knew that I was onto something here: I had a perfect circle inside a pentagram. Now, I don't personally practice witchcraft, but I know that witches cast a circle to do their spells in. So a circle inside a pentagram gave me the impression that this was an important place. The question was why was it so important?

I leaned back on the boulder in the center, and closed my eyes. The dream began suddenly, and I never had a chance to avoid it.

CHAPTER 3:

UNEXPECTED VISITOR

Time seemed to become elastic once the dream began. Minutes or hours, I don't know, but everything blurred and I found myself back in the clearing. It was the same clearing, I recognized the shape, but it looked very different; the stone piles and the boulder were missing. A figure dressed in a peasant shirt and breeches came tripping into the forest.

The man was breathing very hard as if he'd been running, and bent at the waist to catch his breath. I'd never seen a picture of him, but I was pretty sure that this was Icabod Crane. He kept glancing over his shoulder and jerking at every small sound. It was easy to see that he was scared of something that he was trying to out run.

When the crash of brush echoed through the clearing, I had a pretty good idea who was coming. But, I have to admit that when the horseman broke through the tree line, I jumped. I knew instinctively that the headless figure before me was actually my how-ever-many-greats grandfather, but I was still scared.

I tried to run and stop what I knew was coming next. But I couldn't get there.

In a lightening fast move, the horseman swung out with his arm grabbing Crane and throwing him to the ground. The horse reared and those thrashing hooves came crashing down on the huddled body; again and again and again.

When the sound stopped, I opened my eyes. The horseman had dismounted and was now dragging the body. I could see where he was going; a small opening in the earth that was largely overgrown with vegetation. He tossed the body into the small cave, and pushed a large rock into place. He rearranged the vegetation and studied his work, before he remounted his horse and rode off into the forest.

Ferns at the edge of the clearing began waving in the non-existent breeze. There was a faint light, and then she emerged from behind the oak. She was dressed in a plain black dress, with a bonnet tied over her head. She walked into the clearing with her eyes closed and a hand outstretched. I knew her as the witch who had cast the curse; I'd seen her here in my dreams before.

She walked as if she was being guided and with a casual flick of her wrist, the rock at the entrance of the cave flew away. She reached in an pulled out the body. Collapsing to the ground she tenderly rubbed the wounds that had been caused in the attack. But he was too injured, and she held him as he died.

Her body shook with grief as she mourned him.

When she stood, she moved with the confidence of someone who was sure of their decision and what had to be done. Moving to the clearing she stood in the very center, and throwing her arms out cast her circle.

Fire erupted in blue and white flames, circling her. As her voice began to grow, so did the flames. The earth shook and a boulder pushed its way to the surface of the earth. A wave of her hands brought more stones to the clearing. She chanted in a language that I didn't know as she moved the earth and stone to create what I now realized was a shrine to her great nephew, Icabod Crane.

The chanting stopped, the flames dwindled down to just a glow on the ground. She reached under her cloak and pulled out a knife with one hand and a necklace with the other. Saying some words in the same language as before, she drew the knife across her palm let the blood drip onto the medallion that swung from the necklace and smeared more onto the boulder that now occupied the center of the clearing.

The circle of flames now went out, and only a black ring now surrounded her. She strode through the ring, going back to the body. She tossed the necklace inside the mouth of the small cave and with a flash of light, she and the body disappeared.

Intense as it had been, the image faded as fast as it had come. My senses picked up the cracking of a branch not too far from where I was. There was no time to do anything. Suddenly, there was something warm and soft pressing down on my lips. My eyes shot open with alarming speed, and my hands were already pushing whomever it was off.

"Stevie," I heard Ian's voice. "I'm sorry, I shouldn't have done that."

I looked over at the shape on the ground. The adrenaline that was pumping through my body must have over worked my senses, focusing only on flight or fight response as opposed to taking inventory of what was happening. "Ian! What are you doing here?"

Ian sat up, looked at me and smiled. "I was trying to give myself some room away from you, actually. When we saw each other in the hall, before I could say anything you had taken off running, and I had no idea where you had gone. You didn't come to lunch, so I became more and more frustrated and decided that it was time to sign out of school for a little bit, and came here. Here, where I find you looking like Sleeping Beauty, so I woke you with a kiss."

I smiled, "And got knocked on your butt for your effort." I held out my hand to help him up. "I'm sorry I hit you. I thought that I was alone out here, and must have dozed off."

Pulling my jacket tighter around me gave me something to do with my hands to help hide the nervousness that I now felt. "Ian, I'm glad that you came out here today. There is so much that I think we need to talk about. I need to know where we are right now."

"It appears that we are somewhere at the edge of the park, in a clearing."

"No, Silly, I'm talking about us. A week ago, we were in a committed relationship. We had a fight because I was an idiot, we broke up, worked together to stop an attack on a mutual friend. But I need to know where we are now? Are we talking to each other, friends or is there a chance of getting back to what we had?"

Ian smiled, "You've been on my mind since that moment I walked out of your shop. But I figured you needed time to get your thoughts together before we could try to put things right. I love you, Stevie. There's a part of me that has always felt that there was something kind of magical between us."

I grabbed him around the neck and pulled him close. The tear in my heart closed and I felt more confident and ready to handle things that were coming.

Once our lips touched, the heat flowed through my body faster than if it had been in my veins. Our bodies rubbed together and a whole new sense of urgency swept over me. Only upbringing slowed us down. "Ian," I said between kisses, "I think we should take a little step back here."

"Hmm?"

"We can't do this here and now," I said a little stronger.

Revelation struck him. "Oh. I'm sorry. I got a little carried away." He took a step back, but didn't release my hand. "So, what is so special about this place?" he asked to change the focus.

"I think that it is some kind of shrine, that Crane's aunt built for him."

"Not exactly what I would have envisioned for a shrine. Wait. How do you know that she built it for him?"

I spent the next ten minutes telling him about my dream. How this was the place where the Headless Horseman had killed Icabod Crane, and where the body had been originally placed. I finished my tale with the description of how the witch had created this area.

Ian looked at me in disbelief. "Do you really think that she did all that?"

"I don't know. What I do know is that during the last quest, I had several very realistic dreams, and when I awoke it was as if I'd been there. If there was rain in the dream, I'd wake up wet. There was almost always a fire in the dream, and I always smelled smoke when I first woke."

"It's weird, you know that you're finding out information on the other level. Makes me wonder what's going on."

I laughed, "I've been wondering that for the past six months. If you find out, can you copy me on the memo?"

His eyes sparkled and he had that mischievous grin. "Sure. Now, where did you say that the cave was?"

"Just typical. You think the information is suspect, but you still want to check it out." When he said nothing, I shrugged, "It's over here."

A minute later, we were fighting our way through the overgrown brush. I didn't so much see the cave, as step into it. But once we found it, we didn't dare go in.

Ian leaned over and looked in, "It's a bit too dark to see much in here beyond the first few feet." He stepped out of the way so I could see. I slipped on a moss-covered rock, and proceeded to fall head first into the gaping hole.

"You know, Stevie, if I'd known that you really wanted to go spelunking, I'd have brought a flashlight."

"Oh, ha-ha," I said as I tried to push myself to my feet. My hand hit something metal. "Um, Ian? I think I found it."

"Found what?"

"I think I found the medallion that she threw in here."

I felt his hand grab my arm, "Ready?" he asked and then he pulled me back into the sunlight.

Mud was caked onto the surface, but it scraped away easily enough. "Look! It looks just like the other two medallions that I found before."

Ian looked at the medal, "Yeah, it does." He frowned for a second and squinted, "What's this down here?" he asked pointing to some kind of symbol at the bottom.

I looked at it. "I don't know. I don't think I've seen it on either of the others. But to be honest, I didn't look either."

"Well, why don't we head there and we can take a look at the three together."

"I guess that might work. Wait. Wait time is it?"

"School should be letting out in about fifteen minutes. Besides, they probably called home to confirm your appointment."

"Oh no," I groaned. "If my mother finds out that I cut out, she's going to kill me."

"You could always tell the truth."

I tried to glare at him, but decided that he was probably right. As we walked back to the clearing, I pulled out my phone, and confessed all. It turned out that the school hadn't called yet, but while I was on the phone with my mom, the house phone rang and we heard the message being left that they were in fact confirming my appointment. "I'll cover for you this time, Stevie, but let's try not to skip school."

"You looked relieved," Ian, said when I got off the phone.

"She took it better than I anticipated. In fact, she's going to cover for me. What are you looking at?" I asked when I noticed that he was intently eying the medal.

"I'm not sure. This shape on the bottom part there looks vaguely familiar, but I really can't put my finger on it right now."

"Well, let's head home, and we can look at it with better lighting and magnifying glasses. He took my hand and we walked away from the clearing.

Feeling the warmth of Ian's hand in mine let me concentrate on what good had come out of today. I was able to forget the comments that Gabby and Tanya had made, or the threats of Tony's two goons. For whatever it was worth, I felt like my life was getting closer to being back on track. And most of that was due to Ian being a part of my life.

We walked back to the car in silence. He would squeeze my hand every few minutes and I just smiled back at him. When we reached his old rusted car, he acted the gentleman in every way holding the door open for me.

As we headed back down Bedford Road, he turned to me. "I forgot to ask when we were in the woods there, what happened with the new clue this morning?"

I blushed, "Oops. I'm sorry, but since I didn't know where we stood this morning, I didn't think to mention it. And thinking of it now, just made me realize that I didn't let Chrissy know either." By the time that we had turned off of Sleepy Hollow Road, I'd filled him in, and had texted Chrissy about my box of confetti.

"So you think it's some kind of jigsaw puzzle?" he asked.

"That would be my best guess. There are some pieces that have smooth curved edges to them, but most of the pieces have tab or indents where it looks like they could be locked together.

"Well, that sounds like a puzzle all right. Good thing I love puzzles."

"Are you referring to the jigsaw or me?"

He laughed and ran his fingers through my hair. "Stevie, you truly are a puzzle that I love. But in this case I meant the jigsaw.

He pulled his car into the driveway behind my mom's car and we headed in. I couldn't help but notice how things that had seemed to overwhelm me this morning weren't having the same effect on me now. I opened the door and stepped into the warmth and smell of Mom's cookies.

Mom came to the door, "Ah, here are two likely delinquents."

"Mom, I, um I'm sorry. It was just the way that some of the kids were treating me. I needed some space."

"It's lucky for you that I can understand that. Come on in, have some cookies before you go to work." She turned to Ian, "Hi, Ian. It's good to see you. I'll get an extra plate ready. I made kiss cookies, and she doesn't share."

By the time he'd managed to say, "Thanks, Mrs. Nixon," she was already gone.

I was coming home from a horrendous day, had my boy friend with me and was getting ready to gorge on my favorite cookie. If I could end it there, I'd say that at this exact moment, all was well in life. But for me, the medal we'd found today coupled with the dream that I'd had, reminded me that my life was on the line.

CHAPTER 4:

HELP

Ian and I plowed our way through the plate of cookies and a few glasses of milk before Kyle walked in. "What are you doing home already?" he demanded.

"It's a long story, Kyle, and right now we don't have time to do the play-by-play. So we can just say that things happened at school today and I ended up coming home early."

"Boy, how can I get that once in a while?" he asked as he grabbed a handful of cookies from the tray and headed for his room.

I led Ian upstairs and we went to my Mom's office. I
knocked and went in when she called. "Mom, would it be okay if
I showed Ian the clue? I told him about it, and he's worked on
the others, but this one's a bit hard to explain."

"Are you planning to take it downstairs?"

"No. I think that it would be better if it stayed out of harms
way. I mean those pieces are so small and we don't know what
will happen if anything gets lost. I thought that we could work
on it in my room. We'd leave the door open so you could pop in
any time"

She thought about it for a moment. "I suppose that it's okay.
Is anyone else coming over?"

"I'm not sure right now. I'll probably give them a call in a
little while, so maybe they'll come over. I can let you know."

"Okay. Have fun."

We started back down the hall to my room. "Have fun," I
muttered. "I absolutely hate doing this kind of puzzle."

Ian wrapped his hand around my waist and tugged gently.
"If we're together, we can make it fun."

Reaching my room, we propped the door open and I led him
over to the desk. I pulled out the box and took the top off and let
him look at all of those little pieces. While he was immersed
there, I called Emily and Chrissy. Perhaps he was good with
puzzles, but I also knew that the two of us alone in my room

could get in a lot of trouble. The best defense there was to share the wealth by calling our friends.

"Emily said she'll be here in about fifteen minutes and Chrissy will be here after she runs a couple of errands for her mom. She figures no longer than forty five minutes."

Ian looked up from the box, "Okay, we should be able to make that work. Do you want to get started on putting this together now, or should we wait until we are all here?"

I thought about this for a few minutes while I started out the window. "I think that it might be better if we waited. Right now, I'm not even sure where we can put this together. I mean, we don't even know how big it is or anything."

"That's true," Ian conceded as he came up behind me. We'll figure something out." He spun me around so I was facing him, and the mischievous grin disappeared. "You've got something serious on your mind. What's up?"

"Ian, I've got something that I've been pondering all day, and I'm hoping that I can perhaps get your take on it."

"Sure. What is it?"

"I'm trying to figure your cousin out."

He laughed out loud, "You and almost every adult in the family."

"No, what I mean is, yesterday when we all went out for pizza, she was nice to everyone. Today in school she's verbally bashing you and me. I don't get it. Then as if that's not enough, I'd swear that when she thinks nobody is around, she looks incredibly sad and worried about something."

Ian pondered this for a moment and stared to the window while he organized his thoughts. "I'm not really sure what's going on with her. When I see her at family gatherings and stuff, she doesn't act like she does at school most times. I'm not sure if that's because my aunt would kill her or if she's putting on some big act while we're at school trying to make her more popular. Personally, I think the truth is closer to the second idea."

I nodded, as that was one of the possibilities that I'd come to earlier in the day. I felt better having someone who knew her better come to the same conclusion.

Twenty minutes later, Emily strolled in carrying a few bags. "Got some supplies to help us while we're solving puzzles."

"Whatcha got?" Ian asked.

I looked on in wonder as she pulled out two six packs of cola and a box of swiss cakes. Ian and I looked at the cakes and then each other with slight grimaces.

"What," Emily asked noting our expressions. "Do neither of you like swiss cakes?"

"It's not that Em, I swear. When we got here, my mom stuffed us with kiss cookies."

Emily looked at Ian. "You got a kiss cookie?"

He wasn't sure what to make of how she asked this. "Um, more than one actually."

"Wow. It must really be love. She never shares those. With anybody. Ever. I think you may be the first on that score."

I whacked her arm, "Okay, enough about my cookie fetishes. I think we should get started on this."

"Oh! I brought something for that too!" she said quickly. She grabbed her bag and extracted a few cheap disposable plastic bowls. "I figured that we could separate all the parts and then go from there."

There was a knock on the door, and we turned to see Chrissy standing there. "Did I miss anything?" she asked.

"Nothing but finding out that Stevie shared kiss cookies with Ian."

"Wow! She must really be in love with him, huh?"

I rolled my eyes and Ian just laughed.

Standing around my desk, we were all looking at the pile of confetti that was in the box. "This looks impossible," Chrissy stated. "They didn't even give you a picture of what it' supposed to look like when we're done."

"Well, I don't think that they could realistically give me a picture. If they did, I'd have the clue, so why solve it?"

We began the arduous task of separating the pieces. We used four bowls: ones that had curved edges, ones that were all black, ones that were all white and ones that were a mixture.

"I've got a feeling that this is going be to a lousy picture," Emily said. "There is only black and white. There isn't even any gray, or varying shade of black."

"Maybe this is like the first clue," I offered. "You know where we had to not only translate the words, we had to put them in an order that allowed the clue to become clear."

"I suppose that makes sense," Ian added.

Looking at the bowls that now covered my desk, I wondered how we were every going to do this. "There has to be well over a thousand pieces here. Obviously, we aren't going to be able to put it all together in one night. How am I going to keep this together, without losing any thing?" Even I could hear that my voice was rising in pitch, signaling the onset of a panic attack. Luckily, Ian took control.

"Stevie," he said while gripping my shoulders. "We'll figure out the solution to each problem as they arise. Yes, you've got a few valid points, but I'm sure that if we put the four of us together, we can find a creative solution. We just need to brainstorm here."

I stopped shaking. Ian looked at me, right in the eyes. "Look at me, Stevie. Right here, look into my eyes. Now, breathe; in and out. Again."

In a matter of minutes, I had calmed down to a point that I could sit with out visibly shaking. "Okay, let's figure out the answers to those questions, so I can avoid another attack like that," I told everyone.

Finding a way to store the puzzle when not in use turned out to be easier than I thought. Mom had heard the start of my panic attack, and had listened while I got calmed down before she came in. "The easiest thing to do with the puzzle, is to roll it," she said.

"Roll it?" I asked.

"Sure. If you place a large piece of fabric down first and do the puzzle on the fabric. When you are done for the day, you just simply fold the other end over and roll it up. We could even put a tie on it so it can't unroll on you."

"Wow, that's a great idea, Mrs. Nixon," Emily said and both Chrissy and Ian nodded.

The second problem was a little harder for me. "We're still dealing with over a thousand pieces," I reminded them.

Ian found the answer to this one. Placing his hands on my shoulders he said, "Stevie you're going to do this the same way you'd eat an elephant."

"Yuck! Why would I want to eat an elephant?"

"It's a metaphor. The way you'd accomplish that is to do it one bite at a time."

"Okay, so I do it like building the plane." I could relate to that. "Only problem is there aren't any instruction."

Putting the puzzle together on the piece of material that my mom had pulled from her sewing room took much longer than I had ever imagined. We worked on it for better than two hours, and it was slowly taking shape, but we had yet to get the entire outer edge completed.

Mom called us to dinner around six. Without us knowing it, she had made arrangements for everyone to stay for dinner. As we gathered around the table in the dining room, it seemed that everyone was talking at once. Kyle was going on about how track practice was going. Mom and Dad were discussing some business matters. I looked down the table and saw Chrissy and Emily discussing what sounded like fashion.

I nudged Ian, who was to my left, "It's been one crazy day today."

"Yeah, I guess."

"You've been quiet tonight, anything that you'd like to talk about?" I asked.

"I've been thinking about what we talked about earlier. You know, about Gabby and the way that she's been acting? I've got this strange feeling that there is something going on that once we pry the lid off , so to speak, is going to be so huge that it's going to be a life changing experience for all of us."

I tapped my foot on the chair leg while I thought. "You might be right. The whole idea that her actions may be tied to her trying to act a part might also be construed as her trying to cry out for help."

Retreating back to my room after dinner, we did a little more work on the puzzle, at least until Misty decided to come for her visit. "Come on, Misty, jump up here," I patted the cushion of the window seat next to me, hoping that if she'd come up, the others could roll up the puzzle and get it out of harm's way.

Misty wasn't exactly interested in coming up by me right at this exact point, and I didn't know why until Ian flopped down on my bed and the dog started pawing at his shirt pocket.

"Is this what you want, you screwy dog?" he said pulling out a Milkbone.

In answer, her little stub of a tail went into overdrive. She was wiggling so much that I thought that she might just knock herself over.

"Well," Emily said as she took the seat next to me, "it looks like we're about done for tonight at least."

"Yeah. Misty seems to think that the time right after dinner is only for play. So she's going to be demanding my attention for the next hour or so."

Chrissy had walked over and joined our conversation, "But taking a break isn't such a bad thing. We made good progress on the puzzle tonight. Now you let it go for a while and then work on it tomorrow."

I watched as Ian started playing tug-of-war with Misty and her battered chew toy. "The problem is, there is still a deadline coming up. Granted, we've got just about three months, but it's still there on the horizon. We spent nearly three hours, with four of us working on this tonight, and we still don't have the perimeter done yet. I'm just getting concerned; we've got a long way to go before we can even start to decipher the clue."

Both of the girls rubbed my shoulders.

Talking with everyone kept me calm, and it was Ian who had a good suggestion. "Why don't we start looking at our free times? If we can arrange it with your mom, Stevie, perhaps we can work on this whenever one or more of us has some free time."

"I'm not following you," I said.

"Do you think your mom would be opposed to letting one of us in so we could work on the puzzle while you were doing something else?

"But I'm supposed to solve it," I whined now.

"Stevie," Emily said, "nobody is trying to take that responsibility away from you. I think what Ian is suggesting is that if we can each put a little extra time in here, we can get the puzzle ready for you, so you can solve the clue."

"Bingo!" Ian said. "You yourself keep saying that you're not the best with jigsaw puzzles, but some of us like them. Let us use our strengths to help get you ready for whatever it is that comes next."

I thought about it. "I'll check with my mom. Maybe we can find a place in the family room and go from there.

Chrissy and Emily headed out less than fifteen minutes later, each armed with a list of times that they would be coming over to work on the puzzle. It was left that if I was available when they were here, I could help if I chose to. It was nice, but a little weird.

Grabbing our coats, Ian took my hand and led me out into the spring night air. We followed the path towards my shop, and then veered off and headed towards a little bench that my dad had put out here for my mom. We stopped and Ian pulled me in and kissed me.

"I love coming out to look at the stars," he commented. "But tonight I can see the brightest of them all right here with out craning my neck."

"Where?" I asked.

"I'm looking at you, Silly." He tapped my nose.

"You're a sap who really needs to have his eyes checked."

"Nope. Pretty sure I've got the prettiest girl in the town right here, wrapped in my arms."

"Well, I can't agree on the prettiest girl part. But being here wrapped in your arms is exactly where this girl wants to be."

I just let him hold me. Feeling the warmth of his embrace and accepting the strength of friendship. We shifted from standing by the bench to sitting on the bench cuddled together. Together, we watched the stars twinkle and enjoyed our quiet time alone.

Rubbing my hands together I looked at Ian, "I think maybe we should head back to the house. My nose is numb and I'm losing feeling in my fingers."

"Probably right. I don't want to, but I think if we stay out here much longer, we're going to freeze." He stood and extended a hand down to me to help me up.

As we walked back to the house, our hands were still linked, and our arms were swinging back and forth. He started humming a song that I didn't recognize. "What song is that?" I asked.

"It doesn't have a name yet."

"Yet?" I asked.

"It's one of those things that happens when I'm with you. I get this feeling, and it's almost like my soul wants to sing. But since I'm so musically inept, I just hum."

"Oh. So this is how you feel when you're with me?"

"Yeah. I'm trying to work with a friend of mine who plays piano very well, and have him figure it out so we can record it. It could be fun."

"So would that mean that I would actually have a song that was written about me?"

"That's the plan."

We had reached my house, and I knew that it was about time for me to go back in and Ian to head home. "Ian, that's flattering. I can't wait to hear it. Now maybe I'll have to see if I can make one up for you."

"Don't worry about that. Right now you've got enough on your plate. Although, there is something that I wanted to talk to you about."

My eyes narrowed, as I looked at him, suspicious of what was coming next. "Okay. What is it?"

Swinging me around, he pulled me in close and kissed me once more. "Stevie, I was wondering if you would consider going with me to the prom in June?"

The prom? I'm here worried about getting through the next clue, and he's thinking about the prom. But then the girl in me kicked up. "Yes. I'd love to. I'm just a little surprised that you asked when it's still three months away."

"I know it's a ways off, but I'm thinking that by giving you the chance to get ready for the next three months, you won't be having a major panic attack in the middle of June."

"Yeah, I sure don't need any extra stress in my life at that point. But, this will give me something to look forward to when things start to get me down with this next clue.

He pulled me in for a hug, and then we shared a long, warm-your-toes kiss. "I'll see you in the morning," he said. He kissed my hand just before he walked away.

"Ian," I called. When he turned, I smiled and said simply, "I love you."

CHAPTER 5:

SURPRISE

Days flew by in what seemed an endless rush of repetition. Get up, go to school, work on the puzzle, go to bed. By the time I'd been at this for three weeks, I was incredibly weary of it. I wanted it to be done, but the puzzle was far from finished.

It may seem like three weeks would be a very long time to work on a single puzzle, but this was no ordinary puzzle. We had no idea on how many pieces it had, but there were a bunch. The pile of pieces never seemed to get any smaller; I even started to wonder if the blasted things regenerated when no one was looking.

Then to complicate the whole matter, the pieces were black, white or a combination of those two colors. Without a picture to work from it was hard to guess which all white piece went where. All I had to do was step into the family room and look at the rolled fabric that held what we had done to date, and I got an immediate headache. I needed a break.

At lunch that day, I looked at my friends who sat with me, "I've got an announcement. I want to take today off from working on the puzzle."

Emily set her milk down slowly, "What? We can't afford to take days off right now."

"Em, I thank you for all of your help on this, but I've hit the point that if I don't take a little time for me, I think I'm going to go postal."

"That makes sense," Ian said. "What are you thinking of doing?"

I shrugged my shoulders. "Not sure. But whatever it is, I can assure you that it won't involve working on a jigsaw, or trying to guess where a piece goes."

Hours later, as I flipped through my copy of the plans for my plane, I was in shock. Most of the big parts were now done. I'd looked ahead and had already made the parts that I would need once I was able to get the whole thing moved to the hangar at Poppy's airport. So, it appeared that all that was left was to run some wires for the instruments and the electrical system, and to build the engine.

I looked at the crate that sat in the corner or shop where Dad and I had put it right after my birthday in August. Poppy had smiled when I opened my package from him. It's not every day that your granddaughter is ecstatic because you'd given them a package that included all of the parts to build the engine for her plane. But I'd squealed like a little girl when I pulled the tarp back and saw it.

Now, it was the last thing for me to build so I could finish my plane.

I sighed and went over to the large box and pulled. Nothing. There was no way that I was going to be able to move this box without help. So I could either call for help, or I could just open it and remove each part individually.

It took me about an hour to get all of the parts moved to my main work area. I took a quick inventory of everything and then opened the instruction manual.

Thoughts of what I'd said at lunch came back. I'd said that I didn't want to spend the time trying to figure out where each piece went. Well here I was surrounded by parts, trying to figure out where each part went. At least there hadn't been any major surprises with this so far. The instruction book was excellent and included enough pictures that made part identification almost easy.

I tried to keep my mind on the exact task that I was working on, but time and again thoughts of the witch's puzzle sneaked in. Two questions kept popping into my head. Why couldn't I have been given a simple picture or at least better instructions? Why did I have to look at each piece one at a time and decide how it was going to make the whole?

I looked at the next step of the plane-building process, and wondered how Mom was going to take it when I walked in to 'bake' a few pieces. Apparently the way to get the shrink hubs on was to heat them up, so they'd expand, and then slip them on while still hot. As they cooled, the theory was that they would contract to form a nice tight fit.

Glancing up at the clock on the wall, I was surprised. "How did it get to be so late?" I wondered out loud. Normally we'd have dinner around six-thirty, but here it was going on eight. I decided that I'd probably be best off if I called it a night now, and then I would spend a little time after dinner working on the puzzle. I'd feel less guilty if I could tell everyone that I'd spent an hour on it after dinner.

I started putting my tools back on the tool board, humming quietly along with the radio. I'd been so lost in my own thoughts that I dropped a wrench that I had in my hand when I was startled by the knock at the door.

Looking over at it, I figured that it was someone from my family coming to tell me that dinner was ready. "Come in," I yelled.

The door stayed closed, although I thought I heard some movement on the outside. Now I was starting to freak myself out. "Who's there?" I asked timidly, and picked up one of the mallets from my metal table. With the mallet raised, I slowly walked towards the door, making as little noise as I could.

Suddenly the door opened, I shrieked and dropped the mallet on my toe.

"That's an interesting welcome, Stevie. How about helping me in so I can take a look at this place," Aunt Nancy asked.

"Aunt Nancy! I didn't know you were coming!" I squealed as I ran over to help her maneuver her wheel chair through the door.

"Well, I had a little time coming, so I decided that I'd come see you and the rest of the gang for the holiday."

"This is the first time that I can remember you being here for Easter. I can't wait for you to see everything that is going on."

Aunt Nancy is my dad's younger sister, and she is my favorite relative. We've been close for as long as I can remember, even longer if the pictures are any indication.

Nancy had chestnut hair that was kept bobbed just below her jaw line. Her green eyes peeked out from thick-framed glasses, and she maneuvered her wheelchair as deftly as most people walked.

Nancy hadn't always been in the wheel chair. It had only been the past five years. I ran my left hand over my right arm and felt the scars that the accident had left there as well.

Memories flooded back and for a brief second I was back in that car riding with Aunt Nancy. We'd taken the train into New York City to see a matinee showing of *Wicked*, and we were on the way back from the train station in Tarrytown. We had just turned onto Beekman Avenue on the way home, when a drunk driver crossed over the center line. Aunt Nancy tried to avoid the impact, but we still got hit nearly head-on. The momentum of the crash took us all into a telephone pole which collapsed onto the cars. The drunk was killed when the pole smashed through the roof of his truck, and Nancy had suffered a broken back. I remember seeing the truck veering into our path, Aunt Nancy and I screaming, the sound of the twisting metal as the two vehicles melded into one mass and then hitting my head on the door when we hit the pole. I vaguely recall the pole coming down on top of me.

The next memory I have is of waking up in Phelps Memorial Hospital Center. I'd been in a coma for nearly a month. It was only when I asked where Nancy was that every one grew silent and I'd feared the worst. It was a relief to find out that she was also still in the hospital, but the reality of the situation was that the crash had severed her spinal cord in her lower back and that my fun loving aunt would never walk again.

Rolling herself around the main part of the fuselage, she looked at what I had constructed. "It looks beautiful, Stevie. Has Poppy been out here to give it a good going over?"

"Yeah. He and Tom have been out several times. They both have given everything their seal of approval."

"I'm amazed at how fast you've done all of this. Going to school, building a plane from scratch, and if what I hear from Scott is right, you have a boyfriend as well. You've been busy."

"My dad likes to needle me about everything. But, yes, I do have a boyfriend. His name is Ian. Ian Morris, and he moved to Sleepy Hollow back around the beginning of the school year."

"So, what's he like?"

Now I was getting a bit embarrassed, "He's sweet, thoughtful and patient. He's had some rough times in his life, but he's figured out how to get through things fairly well. He's smart. We actually met in our AP Physics class."

"Why don't you finish cleaning up, and then you and I can go get some dinner and you can fill me in on the details?"

"That sounds good," I sighed. "There are some other things that I think I'd like to talk to you about, Aunt Nancy."

She watched me as I scurried around putting everything back where it was supposed to go. "Perhaps you'll tell me what is really eating at you."

I turned and stared at her for a minute. How was she able to be so perceptive? "Wh-what do you mean?"

She laughed a loud, bark of a laugh. "Stevie, my dear, I've always been able to read your expressions. I can tell that right now there is something that is very trying that is bothering you. Actually, I'm thinking that there is more than one problem that you are dealing with. So, be honest with me, tell me the whole story and let me see if I can help. Remember, I've had my share of dealing with adversity."

"Yeah, you have. And you are right, there are a few things that I'm trying to deal with right now that almost seem impossible to handle."

We took Nancy's rental car to the restaurant since it was equipped for her, and had a place for her wheel chair. As the car bounced along, I tried to think of the best way to open up to her about the curse, Gabby and how everything seemed to be piling up on me right now. I didn't have to wait too long.

"So, Stevie, your dad tells me you've been doing a little genealogy and found out some interesting information about the legend of your little town."

How did she do that? She zoomed right in on the topic that I was struggling with. "Yeah. It's a bit complicated, though."

"Well, why don't you tell me what you can? If I've got questions, I'll ask."

I let out a long sigh. "Well, here goes nothing, then," I said and then proceeded to tell her the long tale of the mysterious box, the curse and what I'd found.

"So, let me see if I've got this right. We are descendants of the guy who created the headless horseman, and Icabod Crane's family has basically put a hex on us?"

Closing my eyes, I nodded. "Yeah, that's pretty accurate. Truth be told, the whole idea of that legend being true scares the heck out of me. And the thought of the price of failure seems a bit too high for my likes as well."

We had just pulled into the parking lot, and were sitting in the car. She killed the ignition and we sat for a minute. "Stevie, let's face it. There are no clear guarantees in life, except for taxes and death. You're facing what seems to you to be a quest of insurmountable odds. You're focusing on what happens if you don't succeed. What would happen if you didn't try at all?"

"We wouldn't be having this conversation. They would have buried me back around Christmas."

"Okay, so you made a choice to push through, and gave it your all. And you won. You've beaten this curse twice already, and now you're setting up to make the grand slam. Don't let up on this." She paused and stared out the window for what seemed to be a long time. "Stevie," she said quietly. "I've never shown this to anyone else. It's not from fear that they wouldn't approve of it, but because they didn't need to see it. I think you do."

I stared at her. What hadn't she shown anyone? "Huh?" was my brilliant response.

She turned in van's seat, so she was closer to facing me, and pulled up her left pant leg. There was an angel tattooed there with the words, "Live the Dash" underneath. "Aunt Nancy, when did you get a tattoo?" I asked.

"I got this the year I moved to Scottsdale. After the accident, and the number of surgeries that followed, I'd started losing hope. Here I was rapidly approaching the big four-oh, my marriage had ended when your Uncle was killed in Iraq. I had no kids, and now I was paralyzed. Talk about being a real downer. There were nights I'd lay in the hospital and think about just pulling the plug."

I stared at her; I'd never heard her talk like this.

"Luckily for me, there was a nurse that worked nights. Joan came in to see me one day and we talked about what I was going through. When she came the next night, she brought me a copy of a poem by Linda Ellis, titled *The Dash*. After reading it, my attitude began to change. Instead of dwelling on what I'd lost, I started looking at how I was going to do things to leave my mark. I think that that poem probably saved my life. When I went out to Scottsdale to start over, I decided to get this. I look at it every day to remember that I can make a difference, and that people will remember me for what I accomplish."

I was too stunned to say anything. I reached over and hugged her. I knew that I was going to have to get a copy of that poem. Perhaps I'd even consider getting the same tattoo.

Everyone had always talked about the great little Italian restaurant, DeMarco's, so I was quite excited to have a chance to finally go there. Walking up the ramp behind Nancy, my eyes kept darting left and right to take in the ambiance. Entering the parlor, we were greeted by a woman who was roughly Nancy's age, and then shown to a table. The wait staff was excellent, and had taken drink and food orders quickly, so I sat quietly looking at the pictures on the walls of various places in Italy. I'd always wanted to go there, and had actually planned to go after graduation, but now with the curse hanging over my head, I wasn't sure that was going to be a possibility.

"Aunt Nancy, I'm curious. Why did you decide to take me out to dinner when you just got here?"

She smiled, "It took you a while to get there, didn't it? I call home every few days. When I called a few weeks ago, I could tell that there was something that was bothering my dad, but he wouldn't talk about it. So, I called your dad. I figured if my brother couldn't tell me what was going on, I'd make him feel so bad that he'd find out. Well, it didn't take me long to get him to break on what was going on with you."

"After the whole story came out, he told me how you've been trying to handle it, keep going as if nothing was wrong. But he said that he could see that you were having more issues than you were letting on. I decided right there that I needed to come to see if I could intervene and help you."

Knowing that she had come to help me made me feel special inside. I knew that I could trust her on this, and she would help keep me centered for the next few days while she was here. Having this realization made me feel better about how we had been working on the clues for the last few days.

By the time that we had finished dinner, Nancy and I had talked about almost everything. She wanted to meet Ian, so we were working on a schedule that might work for that.

"Aunt Nancy? I've got one more thing that I'd like your take on if you don't mind." At this point, we were on our way back to Sleepy Hollow.

"Shoot," she said.

"There's this girl at school. We've never been even remotely close as friends, but she seems to be going through a rough spot right now."

"Would this be Ian's cousin, Gabby?"

My head snapped towards her, "How did you know that?"

She laughed. "Stevie, my darling, I know many things. But in this case, I heard the change in your voice when you mentioned her on the ride in. When you told me of the background just now, it was with that same tone."

"Okay, I guess. I'd like to help her if I can, but I don't know how. We have a history of fighting like cats and dogs, so I don't really know how to approach her. I know that Ian says that she is dealing with stuff at home, and in the legal system, and I can't help but think that she could use a friend."

She simply smiled, "I can give you some pointers on this."

CHAPTER 6:

DETERMINATION

We went back to my parent's house and I was surprised when Nancy got out of the car. "I didn't realize that you were coming in," I said while steadying her wheel chair.

"Personally, I don't want to spend the night out here in the car. Could you grab my bags from the back, please?"

"You're staying here?" I asked in a very excited voice.

"Yes. Scott and I talked about it, and since you have a guest room right on the first floor that I can maneuver in and would give me access to be able to help you, it seemed perfect."

I threw my arms around her. "Oh, thank you."

I grabbed her bag from the back of the van and then pushed her up the small ramp that my dad had added years ago that led to the front door.

Once inside, I took her bag to the spare room next to my dad's office while Aunt Nancy went in search of my folks.

Ten minutes later, we were all gathered in the family room, looking at the puzzle that my friends and I had been working on for the last three weeks. Mom and Aunt Nancy both asked if they could spend some time working on it together tonight. It seems that they both really enjoyed doing jigsaws.

Aunt Nancy took control of the conversation. "Well, I got Stevie to tell me a little of what is going on. You were right Scott; she's been hiding how she feels about this scenario more than she'd let on. But, I think we got to the bottom of that, right, Stevie?"

"Um, yeah. It's just hard for me to dump all of this on everyone else. I mean, it doesn't affect them like it does me—"

"Stevie!" my mom snapped. "What do you mean that it doesn't affect the rest of us? Do you have any idea on how much it would tear this family apart if something happened to you? You're our daughter, it would break our hearts if anything happened."

Whoops! "Mom, I know that you guys love me and want to protect me. It's just that if I don't complete this, I'm the one who ends up dead."

"That's right! You'll be gone and we'll be the ones who will have to try to find some way to get through the rest of our natural lives with the gaping hole that would be in our hearts."

Tears now streamed down her face, and my dad pulled her closer, hoping to comfort her. Now I felt guilty.

"Look, I'm doing everything that I know how to do so none of this has to come to fruition. There's a ton of things that I'd really like to do that dying early would screw up." I walked over to them, and hugged them both. "I guess that I'm just so overwhelmed right now."

Dad shifted so he could get one arm around me, "That's why we'd like to help, Honey, if you'd let us."

I felt another arm around my waist and a hand in the center of my back, and realized that everyone in this room would be adversely affected if I didn't succeed. "I'm scared," I admitted to them for the first time.

After the weeping session was over, we sat down and decided that perhaps we could talk some of the process through.

"I think that the first step right now might be to get the puzzle completed," Mom said.

"I agree," I said, "but the problem is that there are so many pieces that looks so similar it is taking forever to do it. And if I'm involved, forget it. I just slow the process down. I can't do it."

"Stevie," Nancy spoke in her quiet voice that she now used to soothe clients in her private counseling practice. "Let's take a step back away from this. I told you earlier tonight about some of my experiences that I had after the accident."

"Do you know how many times I said I couldn't do it? The number of times that I felt that I was just too weak to handle any more physical therapy?"

I shook my head.

"After they got me stabilized, it took a few days before they came in and told me that I'd never walk again. Let's just say that that was a heck of a blow. My plans had never included the possibility of being in a wheel chair for the rest of my life. Then suddenly there I was staring at the next fifty years of never dancing, never being able to get things from the top shelf or a half a million other things that I took for granted."

"Believe me when I say that I wanted to give up. Then I got a little stronger and they started sending me to PT a few times a week. When you can't move a muscle from your waist down and they want you to do all of these things, all you want to do is give up and cry.

"But there is another part of you that you need to find right now. You've seen glimmers of her. She's Stevie the Warrior. She's the part of you that will take the challenge and only concentrate on the positive parts. Right now, you need to find her and let her take the lead."

"But there are so many possibilities," I whined. "How will I know what to do with things?"

Nancy reached over and picked up a few pieces for the puzzle. "Everything that comes into our life is like a puzzle piece. It has a certain color, shape, size or texture. What we need to do is to pick up that piece and hold it in our hands. Turn it around; manipulate it so that we can truly understand what it is. Only then, can we figure out how it's going to fit into our lives.

"Now, we have many choices. We could just ignore certain pieces, and treat them as if they were not important. But what would we have at the end? We'd look at our picture and see that there were holes that marred the surface. We can walk away from the entire puzzle, and then we'll never know what it would show us, or we can find the courage to inspect each piece and complete it. We may not like every piece, but each one is important to who we are."

"I'm not sure I'm following you, Aunt Nancy."

She shifted slightly and took my hands. "Stevie, five years ago, you and I were in the same accident. We both survived and have tried to get back on with our lives. Fortunately, you made a full recovery, but don't you think that the memories of that have affected you in some way?"

"Are you trying to find the positive side of us being hit that night?" I asked incredulously.

"In a manner of speaking, yes. Each piece of this puzzle makes up whom I am. Pieces that have already been used influence us with the next choice that we have to make. For example," she picked up a piece from the bowl. "When you look at this piece, what do you see?"

"It's oddly shaped, and all white."

"Good, now from which pile should I look for the next part?"

"Well, I'd say from the white. But I suppose that it might go with a two-toned piece."

"Exactly. We chose a single piece at random, but then you used your knowledge and intuition to narrow down the most likely choices that came next. Likewise, if I had a piece that showed some black, we probably wouldn't go digging for a white part. Good so far?"

I nodded.

She went on. "Now the more choices we have made the easier some decisions become. For example, if I've found that I have ten pieces that fit together and have left a small opening, I can use the size and the shape along with color to narrow my search. The more pieces I can eliminate means I have a smaller number to chose from, thereby making it easier to choose the right one."

I sat back in the chair. "I think I'm getting it. By not dwelling on things that I can't control, I can focus on things that will improve my dash."

She smiled. "You've got it. It's a change of attitude that will help move you along."

Mom asked, "What do you mean, your dash?"

I must have looked like fish out of water the way my mouth was gaping. Nancy jumped in. "I told her about the poem, "The Dash", when I showed her this." To my surprise, and everyone else's as well, she pulled up her pant leg and showed them her tattoo. This revelation was met with various responses ranging from Kyle's "Cool!" to my mom's "Oh dear, why did you do that?" Dad sat stoically, not commenting either way.

After Nancy shared her story, Mom decided that we should all spend a little time working on the puzzle. When I went to bed just after midnight, everyone else was still down stairs putting it together. They were all laughing and having a great time.

Alone in my room, I sat on the window seat and looked out at the stars. I pondered what Nancy had said about needing to handle each of the pieces of the puzzle of my life. I wondered what my picture would look like.

Sipping from the can of Coke that I'd brought up with me I thought about what pieces my puzzle had. Obviously, there were my friends. They had stood with me throughout this entire quest, and Em and Chrissy had been with me even longer. Ian had obtained a special place in my life; he was my first boyfriend. I started thinking about how my love for flying fit in and how it coupled with my desire to build my own plane. I thought about school and the other students that were there. I could recall several times where I did what I thought was right at the time and didn't worry about the consequences until it was over.

Nancy was right. Each of these experiences had defined the person that I was and helped me shape the way that I would react to each new challenge.

Thinking about my current challenge highlighted new puzzle pieces that I didn't really like and the way that they were being forced to fit into my life. Right now it was very uncomfortable, and they didn't really seem to fit all that well. But, maybe it was a better fit than I realized.

The first clue had been to be honest with all. I thought I had been right up until hours before the deadline when I realized that I was lying to myself about my feelings for Ian. Those lies had kept me from acting on what could be called a piece that didn't fit well then. Now, I never wanted to be without it.

Looking at the second clue, Loyalty, again I had to face something that I was not happy to do at the time, but in retrospect was the right thing for all of us involved. By my standing up for Chrissy, I'd found the leader that was constantly cowering inside of me.

The first two tasks had actually reinforced values that my parents had instilled in me from a very early age. By trusting those values, I made my choices, which influenced how people saw me. And, how I was beginning to see myself.

Now I had one last task. I could either charge towards it or run away from it. Aunt Nancy was right, I needed to find the warrior inside me and make my stand.

My attention was briefly drawn away by the shout that came from downstairs. I wondered what they were excited about. I didn't have to wait long before the door to my room burst open.

"Stevie! We did it! It's all done."

I turned and looked at Mom. Her face was flushed, and here eyes were wild with excitement. "You finished the puzzle?"

"Yep. Nancy and I got talking and things just started falling in place. Come on down and see."

There was another piece that I hadn't even thought about: my family. How they reacted to various things often times influenced my behavior towards something else.

Back in the family room, I walked over to the table where Dad and Kyle were gathered looking at what I assumed was the puzzle.

"Still not sure what it's supposed to be," Dad said.

Kyle tipped his head to one side, "Looks like one of those records that came with the toy record player. You know where the record had a whole bunch of little bumps sticking out that would catch on the player arm to make the music."

I walked around the table and looked. Kyle had been spot on with his description. "Great," I said. "Now all I have to do is find the device to play this on." I looked up at the staring faces. "But, this is the first step of the problem solved. We'll look at the next step tomorrow."

We all agreed, and we went to our rooms. My mind was now trying to figure out how this whole thing was supposed to go together. I sent a text to Ian, Emily and Chrissy to let them know that the puzzle was done. I included a picture, and was not surprised when I got three texts back wondering what it was supposed to be.

I pulled out the three medallions and wondered how they fit together and where they fit in my life. After staring at them for a while, I decided that this was something to ponder in the morning. But for now, I'd just be happy that we'd figured out how the puzzle went together. I closed my eyes with the belief that somehow, I was going to solve this last clue and break this curse forever.

CHAPTER 7:

WEIRD DREAMS

Tossing over and over in bed I finally gave up trying to get to sleep. It seemed that every time I'd think I was settled, I would hear some strange noise and my mind was off to the races trying to guess what it was.

I slipped out of bed and went to the window seat. Curling up on the bench, I reached over and grabbed the heavy blanket that lay on the end of my bed and wrapped it around me. As I had done earlier, I looked out at the stars, and wondered about where things were going with my life.

The answers that I was getting now were the same as the ones that I got earlier. Apparently uncertainty doesn't change with the hour on the clock.

Misty had apparently sensed that I'd gotten up, popped her head up and then plodded over to join me in the window. She crawled up on my lap and nuzzled her head into my chest and let out a heavy breath, kind of like a dog's version of a sigh of contentment.

"You've got it pretty good, Girl," I said while I cuddled her.

Her only response was to shift her head and give me a big doggie kiss.

I guess that I was still trying to rationalize how Nancy could look at the accident that we had both shared five years ago and see any good that came out of it. I knew that two different people would see the same event differently, depending on their frame of mind, but feeling that being in a wheel chair as being good was way out of my comprehension.

I guess that eventually I would get to the point that being "here", even if it meant being in a wheel chair, was preferable to the alternative. Perhaps it was the perspective that came with maturity. I was just twelve when we had had that accident. When I woke, my days were spent trying to get through the nightmares that seemed to follow. Whenever I closed my eyes in those first few days after being in a coma, all I ever saw were the head lights of the truck that hit us. I almost always woke screaming, bringing the nurses. It took quite a while before I was able to make it through the night.

And for the most part, I'd gotten out very lucky. Other than being knocked out for a month, I'd only had bumps and bruises, all of which had healed before I woke.

Nancy would have already been dealing with her injuries for that same length of time. But, she would have been keenly aware of each ache in her upper body and the total absence of feeling in her lower body. Still, she'd found the courage to push through and make it to the other side. And she'd found the compassion to forgive the man who'd been drinking and had put us into that situation.

Somewhere along the thought process, I drifted off to sleep, still sitting in the window.

Mist swirled in the dark night. I was flying above the treetops, I could see the clearing in the distance. The fire there burned bright, illuminating the witch who stood in the center with her arms out stretched.

I fell in a heap on the moist ground near her feet. "So, ye've made it to the final task. It is for this that ye risk ye life. Find those who've known sorrow, give them hope, and see tomorrow." She looked at me and grinned. "Fail and ye shall be here for all eternity." Her laugh was between a cackle and a growl.

"Why do you want me to die?" I cried out. "What did I do to you?"

"What did ye do? You spread the genes of the bastard who killed my dearest. He was murdered because your kin couldn't bear the thought of losing a woman. Now you'll die trying to defend him."

I stood up, and moved towards her. "Von Brunt? He was a jerk. Why didn't you make him pay for what he did? Instead you attack people who weren't even born then. When I got your first message, I didn't even know that I was related to him. Knowing it now doesn't make it better."

"Not my problem, dearie. I only set the curse, it is ye who must fulfill it."

"So you kill innocents if they can't play your sick game. How are you any better than him?"

"It hurts him now better than it could have then. Now, be gone." There was a flash of light and everything spun.

Shades of grays floated in and out of my vision. I saw people that I'd hurt if I failed: Mom, Dad, Nonni, Poppy, Ian, Nancy, Emily, Chrissy. Faces flashed by at an alarming speed; I felt dizzy and fell to the ground.

Searching blindly in the darkness with my hands, I tried to find where I was. I could feel the cold hard floor, and then there was the wiggling furry body of Misty. "It's okay, Girl. I'm here." I thought of the faces that I'd seen; I couldn't let them down. I needed to do what ever it took to break this blasted curse.

CHAPTER 8:

EXCURSION

Misty jumped on me and I startled into something that resembled consciousness. In her excitement, she knocked several things off of the night table. "What's up with you, you silly dog?" I asked her as she hunched down wanting to play. I grabbed my robe and walked to the bathroom with her following me. As soon as I started the water for my shower, she lost interest in what I was doing and curled up with the chew toy that she had carried in.

As the hot water ran over my shoulders, I felt as though my muscles were melting. For the first time in days, I felt relaxed.

Knowing that downstairs, the puzzle that had been taking so much of my time was now completed.

After getting dried and dressed I was about to go down and check out the final product, but I was interrupted by a knock at my door. "Yes?"

"Stevie, Mom wanted me to let you know that she, Dad and Aunt Nancy are going over to Nonni and Poppy's for the day."

"What are your plans, Kyle?" I demanded, hoping that he was going to go somewhere and leave me some alone time so I could relax.

"I'm going to be heading out with some of the guys from the team. There's a new movie playing over at the mall, so that's where we're going. I'll be out of here in about twenty."

Perfect, I thought. That would just leave Misty and me with nothing pressing on the docket.

My phone rang. "Hey, Emily. What's up?" I answered.

"I figured that we've spent enough time on that silly puzzle, and that it was time for you to take a break from it. I was thinking of heading into White Plains and checking out the bookstore and generally bumming around for the day. So, what time should I pick you up?"

"Um, Em? I wasn't planning to go anywhere today. I just kind of figured that I'd hang here and maybe go work on my plane."

"No, you've got to come, Stevie. This trip won't be any fun without you."

I could hear the tone of her voice. It was the one that I always called her river voice; it would just keep pounding you until you gave way. "Okay," I huffed out. "I'm not sure why I've got to go, but if you are so insistent, I guess I'll go. What time were you thinking of leaving?"

"I'll be over in twenty and we'll just go form there."

I disconnected and looked at my phone. How had this happened? One minute I had the entire day free to do as I pleased; now I was committed to going shopping. Not that I really mind shopping, I mean, what girl doesn't? It's just that I'd planned to work on some things to help clear my mind.

Emily actually arrived on time for once, and found me standing in the family room looking at what I had been told was the completed puzzle. It was a circle that was about twelve inches in diameter. The vast majority was plain white. Interspersed along the circle at all variety of locales, small black dots were randomly thrown in.

I had already tried to trace the pattern out, and had played connect he dots. "What's this?" I heard Emily ask.

"This is supposedly the clue. My aunt and my mom just love doing puzzles, and for some reason, which currently escapes me, they got going on this last night when I went to bed. My mom burst into my room around one in the morning to let me know that they had gotten it all together."

"It doesn't look like anything that I even recognize."

"I keep thinking that it reminds me of J.J. Thompson's Plum Pudding model of the atom. That's about the best that I can come up with."

"Well," she finally said, "Let's go hit the mall. This will be here when we get back."

Emily was so excited that her mom was letting her drive the new GMC Jimmy that they had just got, she nearly babbled all the way out to the car. I wasn't exactly sure that a trip to the mall was the best way for her to break the car in, but since it wasn't mine, who was I to argue?

The trip from Sleepy Hollow to White Plains normally took about fifteen minutes. When Emily was driving, the trip took about half that. She liked the idea of flying low. Whenever I rode with her, I would keep my eyes closed for as much of the ride as possible. It was much easier for me to relax if I didn't see the cars flying by.

Today was no exception. She was having too much fun playing with the controls of the new truck, to really pay attention to those pesky things, such as speed limits signs. By the time we got to the mall, I felt ready to kiss the ground in thanksgiving for arriving alive.

Emily almost had to physically drag me into the mall. She was quite obviously energized by our trip; I was still trying to find my land legs. The first store that she went for was Holtzman Jewelers. "Em, what are we going here for?" I asked.

"When I was here with my mom last week, she saw this really cute bracelet. Since her birthday is coming up next week, I figured that I'd pick it up for her."

"Okay, I guess that makes sense." Her logic may have made sense, but I still couldn't figure out why it took us nearly forty-five minutes to get out of there. By the time we'd left, Emily had looked at four rings, two necklaces and had to go back to get the bracelet.

Our next stop was Hahn's bookstore. I've always joked that I wasn't allowed in certain stores without parental supervision, this was one of those places. Whenever I walked into the store, Mrs. Hahn got a big smile on her face. It seemed that I never left without spending over a hundred dollars. Today was no exception as I found three books from my favorite author. By the time that we'd left the bookstore, I was ready to go find a nice quiet corner and try to curl up into one of my new books. This was of course the same time that Emily decided that she needed food.

"I'm starving. What do you think about hitting the food court?"

"I guess I could eat." It wasn't something that was at the top of my list right now, but I knew that I'd be hungry in a little while if I didn't. We meandered through the mall on our way to the food court. My mind was on a trip of its own: vacillating between the new books that I just bought and the puzzle that was waiting for me at the house.

I wasn't even planning for it, or looking for it. But there it was. My prom gown.

The gown was on a mannequin in the display window for Lisa's Formals. "Em. Look at it. It's gorgeous."

Emily looked at me as if I'd claimed that I'd been abducted by aliens. "Stevie, do you even own a single dress? Now, you're standing in front of a window gawking at a prom dress?"

"I'm going in. Coming?" I challenged her.

"When are you going to actually wear a prom dress?" She stopped suddenly. "Ian asked you to the prom, didn't he?"

"Yeah. I never thought that I'd get asked, but this year has been so different. So, he asked, I accepted and now I'm going to look for my dress." I turned and marched into the store, leaving her gaping in the doorway.

"Hi, and welcome to Lisa's, I'm Diane. How can I help you today?" a matronly looking woman said as I cleared the first rack of dresses.

"Um, maybe?" I hesitated, wondering if I should have asked Mom to come. It was too late for that. "I saw the pink gown in the window, and I'm thinking that I need to start thinking about something for my prom."

"Oh, that is a beauty!" She led me toward the side of the store where a rack of dresses hung in a rainbow of colors. "It's more of a vintage style. It has capped sleeves along with a sweetheart bodice. The full skirt has enough poof to make every girl feel like a princess, but not so much that you'll look like you stepped out of a Disney production."

I slowly walked over, and let the material run through my fingers.

"It's made of silk." Diane added. "It's as light as a summer breeze, and feels like a dream. Do you want to try it on?"

I looked over at Emily who was watching me with wide eyes. I nodded, "Yes, I would."

It took three tries before we found one in the right size, but there I stood ten minutes later, looking in the mirror. I could see myself, maybe with my hair pulled up into some mature looking coif, a strand of pearls around my neck and a touch of makeup. Ian was going to drop when he saw me.

"What do you think, miss?" Diane's voice broke into my personal revelry.

"It's perfect." I turned to where Emily was watching. "What do you think, Em?"

She stood with a grin on her face, shaking her head. "What I think is that you must have hit your head pretty hard for you, the queen of blue jeans, to be in here trying on dresses voluntarily. But," she paused and smile, "it's absolutely gorgeous and it is so you."

I beamed at her and looked back at the reflection. I was going to make Ian swallow his tongue. "Can I put a deposit on it now to hold it?" I asked. "My Mom will need to come in to give me the final okay."

"Oh that's not a problem. Let's get you out of it, and we'll go right over here to take care of the paper work."

Before I moved, I had Emily use my phone to get a picture of me in the dress. Once the deposit was paid and the paper work filled out, I sent my mom a text with a copy of the picture. She responded with a "can't wait" and I knew that I would be back within a few days to make the final arrangements.

As we walked out of Lisa's, Emily turned to me, "Now can I finally get something to eat?"

Carrying our few packages, we made our way towards the Food court. As we ambled along, we would occasionally stop to look in a window at some display or other, but we never went inside. We chatted about things that were going on at school, and I tried to bring up a few ideas of the clue.

"Stevie," Emily said a bit frustrated after my latest attempt. "Is there anything that we can do right now about the clue?"

"No," I admitted sheepishly. "The thing is, Em, the puzzle that we thought was the clue doesn't show anything. All we've got is a white circle with black dots."

"Okay, so we don't have much right now. So why don't we take a little bit of a radical approach here? Let's pretend that right now, we are nothing more than two teen-aged girls wandering through the mall having some fun shopping?"

The implied slap was as hard as a physical one would have been. "I'm sorry, Em. This blasted curse has me all tied up and it's obviously making me edgy."

"You sure about that? I thought it was just a bad case of PMS," she said laughing.

She smiled when I laughed with her, and we continued to the other end of the mall and the promise of food.

Rounding the last curve in the hall, we entered into the circular area of the mall where the food court was. Dozens of small establishments lined the walls, and tables were set in the middle of the room making for a large cafeteria styled atmosphere. What set our food court apart from others was what was at the center of the room. We had a carousel, and a fountain.

People, mostly adults, were gathered around the carousel. Most likely watching for their children who were enjoying a free ride. A quick scan of the carousel, and one saw tigers, zebras and elephants that were being ridden by children of all shapes and sizes.

Emily wasn't paying any attention to the carousel, but instead looking for a table that we could claim. When she spotted one, she grabbed my arm and tugged as she sped off toward the newly opened goal.

"Think this will work?" she asked as she dropped her bags onto the extra seat next to her.

"Yeah, this will be fine. Why don't I sit here while you go and get your food?"

Her eyes lit up. "You sure? Thanks!" and she was off to her favorite Chinese place here, Mr. Panda's.

I sat down and scanned the room. I was a little hungry, but I really didn't know what I wanted to eat. My scan went across the fountain that was next to the carousel. Something kept drawing my attention back to it.

I stared at it now. It was a very simple fountain; a large rectangular pool sat on the floor. In the far right corner a rectangular structure poked out of the water to a height of about five feet off of the ground, with a single sinuously curved pole coming form the center that rose another five feet or so.

Water sprayed out of the top of the pole, falling into the small rectangular pool and then cascading down into the main pool at the bottom. Nothing spectacular that was bound to catch my attention.

I watched the spraying water as it toppled through empty space, and thought about a story I'd once heard about Albert Einstein. As he watched the water from a fountain, he moved his fingers in front of his eyes and tried make it appear as though he'd stopped a single drop of water. Tentatively, I raised my hand in front of my eyes and waved it. Immediately, I could see the individual drops better. Now I started trying to wave either faster or slower and the result was that I was almost able to stop a drop.

I was fascinated by this new revelation, and didn't notice other patrons staring at me. I just kept waving my hand.

Then it suddenly worked. Only for a brief second, but it was undeniable: I'd made the water droplets of the fountain stop in midair.

In the midst of my surprise, a thought occurred to me as I looked at the random drops of water that were, for that one, magical moment, frozen.

"Okay, I'll bite," Emily said when she returned and found me standing with my hand directly in front of my face with what had to be a stupid grin on my face,

"I just had a realization," I began. "I was doing something that I'd read that Einstein had done while looking at a fountain. But when I was able to get the instantaneous freeze frame of the water droplets, it occurred to me that maybe this applies to my clue."

"Okay, now you've lost me. Want to try that in English?"

"The experiment here was to cause a strobe effect that made something in motion stop. What if a picture had been taken at that exact moment? All an observer would see would be a series of water droplets that were in one place."

"Okay. I can see that."

"What if my clue was actually that picture? We have the spots on the background. Maybe it is a stop action of some kind and we need to put it into action to be able to see it?

"Stevie," Emily said. "I think you may have gone around the bend on this one, but it is as plausible as anything else. Go grab some food and we can talk about it while we eat.

CHAPTER 9:

ONE STEP FORWARD

Feeling anxious to get home to test my theory, I was ready to go when Emily decided that she wanted desert. "Are you kidding me, Em? You ate two helpings of General Tso Chicken along with half of my nachos and cheese. If I'd eaten like that I'd be on the floor sick as a dog."

"Just because you don't expand your dietary bounds, don't give me a hard time."

"I can't watch," I said. I went back to looking at the fountain, wondering if I'd stumbled onto the basics of solving this clue. I used my phone to shoot a quick video of trying to demonstrate the principal of strobing that was the current cornerstone of my hypothesis.

I noticed a movement on the peripheral of my vision. Naturally, my eyes were drawn towards the movement.

A blonde haired girl was pulling out a chair and huddling into the corner. The hood of the sweatshirt that she wore hid her face. There was something familiar about her, maybe it was the way that she moved or her general appearance, but the little voice in my head said that I new her from somewhere.

"What are you looking at so intently?" Emily asked as she licked hot fudge from her spoon.

"Pestering me isn't going to help my stomach with your eating habits, Em"

"No, seriously, what are you looking at?" she glanced in the direction that I had been looking while she took her seat.

"Do you see the girl over there in the corner, sitting all by herself?" I asked and then waited for her to nod. "There is something familiar about her. I'm just trying to figure why."

Emily laughed. "Stevie, honey, you need to get out more often. Of course she looks familiar; it's Gabby."

"What?" my head snapped to look at the hooded figure again. "I'll be. I guess it is. But is it me, or does she look incredibly miserable?"

Emily looked over as she scooped another mouthful of ice cream. "Well, she doesn't look happy, that's for sure. I wonder what's up."

I made a split second decision. "I'm going to go over to the ATM and grab some cash. That sundae looks better than I thought." I stood up and stated walking over to the cash machine that sat at the far edge of the food court, and not that far from Gabby.

Turning and walking from our table, I went to the far side of the food court and then walked up to the ATM. Swiping my card, I punched in my code and withdrew the forty dollars, which I quickly stuffed into my purse. Taking my receipt, I casually turned and pretended to notice the occupant o the table. "Oh, hi, Gabby. Didn't see you there."

Gabby looked as though she'd been shocked with a high voltage line. "Stevie. What are you doing here? Is Ian with you?" Her voice began to quiver, as if she was nervous.

"No, Ian's not here. Emily and I had a few errands to run, and came over here to get a birthday present for her mom and I ended up doing some dress shopping." I noticed that she was looking extremely pale. "Gabby, are you all right?"

"Look, Nixon, you may be dating my cousin, and we may have hung out a time or two in the past few months, but please don't delude yourself into believing that suddenly you and I are pals."

"It's not that. You just look like something is really eating you."

"Don't worry about me. I'll be fine," she snapped. "I've got to go, I'm meeting someone here, and she just came in."

Stopping only for a minute at the fudge shop to pick up a pound of mint chocolate, I walked back to the table perplexed. "There is something definitely wrong with Gabby," I told Emily. "She looks incredibly pale, and she is still somewhat argumentative, but no where near her norm."

"Any idea who she was meeting with?"

I looked back over at the table where Gabby sat. The woman who was now siting with her was definitely adult. They weren't touching, so I tended to believe that they weren't related in some way. "If I had to guess, I'd say that they know each other on a professional level."

Emily stood and picked up her trash, "Well since you're not eating all of that fudge now, why don't we take off and we can philosophize on the way back."

Bouncing ideas off of each other about Gabby's predicament made the normally short ride home even faster. "I think she's got some family issues," Emily said as we pulled into my driveway.

"I know Ian said there are some things that are going on, but they've been going on for a couple of months. I would think that any issues would have been dealt with over the past few months."

"Yeah, like she had time to do that while she was out belittling our friends and classmates."

I looked over at Emily. "You may have just hit on it," I said. When she only stared at me confused I tried to explain it clearer. "When everything happened back in March with Chrissy at the cemetery, Gabby was the only one that voluntarily went to the police. She even went as far as to plead guilty at the arraignment. I wonder when her sentencing is coming up?"

"Yikes. You're right Stevie, I hadn't even given that a moment's consideration. If she's looking at going to jail for some time, that would definitely be stressful."

"Do you really think that they'll put her in jail? I mean she did turn evidence against the others that were involved. I would think that they'd cut her a little slack, you know, only give her probation or something," I ventured.

Emily shrugged, "I have no idea. But I think it's definitely a possibility."

Admitting that I felt some concern for Gabby was an interesting conundrum that I was experiencing. We'd never been close before, and I wouldn't say that we were now, but for some reason it seemed that she was all-alone now. I thought back to the first time that she and I had crossed paths; Tanya had been there at that point. For as long as I could remember, Gabby and Tanya had been like Frick and Frack; they'd always been a team. But lately, I had seen Gabby several times without Tanya. And for me, that just made the puzzle that much more complicated.

I went into the kitchen with Emily following me. Apparently everyone else was still out. Mom had left me a note that I was to be ready to be picked up around six to go to dinner at my grandparents' house. I looked at my watch; I still had almost four hours.

"Hey, Em, I want to check out the puzzle one more time. I've got a few ideas that I want to look at."

"Does this have anything to do with the way you were flapping your hand at the fountain at lunch?"

Sensing that she truly had no idea on what I was talking about, I decided that I needed to try to show her. "Look," I said as I pulled out my phone. I started playing the video that I had shot, and then paused it a few seconds in. "You know that those drops that we saw were in motion, right?"

"Well, yeah." She looked at me as if she was waiting for some huge revelation.

"Okay, we know that they are in motion, but yet here they are stopped. We can see each one individually. There is no apparent order, but we can see each drop."

"So?"

I pointed over at the puzzle. "The picture on the phone and the picture on the table. I think that they both represent a brief moment in time. A moment when something that was in motion was captured eternally."

"So, you think that the puzzle is like a picture of something that was in motion? How are you going to figure out what it was?"

"I think the whole picture has to go in motion. See the shape, it's a circle. I think it needs to be spun."

"How do you propose to do that?" she asked. "If you spin this puzzle, all of the pieces will fly out and we'll be back at the beginning."

"If I used the actual puzzle, I think you're right. But I had a different idea." I stood on a chair and using my phone, took a picture of the puzzle. "Let's go up to my room and we'll see if we can't make a replica of the puzzle from this. If I can't, then we'll figure out plan B."

We climbed the stairs to my room, with Misty following and we settled in. Emily sprawled out on my bed, while I took the desk chair and began working with the computer. It didn't take very long before we had a fairly good picture on screen. I pressed print and waited for the picture.

"So, how do you plan to spin it?" Emily asked.

"Not a hundred percent sure," I answered. "I'm thinking that I'm going to try for the simple version first."

Planning an experiment and carrying it out in your house is much different than doing it at school. After the page came out of the printer, we went back down to the family room. "I want to compare the two images," I told Emily when she gave me a quizzical look.

I placed the printed page on top of the original puzzle. It looked like the dots matched up fairly well.

"Did you expect something to appear right now?" Emily asked.

"No, I just wanted to make sure that everything is as close as we can get. I know that printers can actually skew objects slightly. Hopefully by reproducing the puzzle we didn't screw anything up with how it translates."

"Oh, now there's a comforting thought."

I laughed. "It looks pretty good," I said, stepping aside so Emily could look.

Walking to the bookshelf on the far side of the room, I picked up some cardboard that we had there. "Think this will work," I said as I returned. I took the printed picture and some spray adhesive from my mom's sewing kit; I attached the paper to the cardboard.

The adhesive dried in less than a minute. "I think we may need to do some trimming," Emily noted. "Look, the cardboard is square, the paper rectangular and the original puzzle is a circle. Just thinking that it would probably be in our best interest to make them all the same shape."

"I hadn't thought of that. Actually, I think we need to take it one step further now that I am thinking along that line. We need to make sure that the center of the puzzle is located at the center of mass."

"The center of what?" she asked.

"The center of mass. When this object spins, it will naturally spin on the center of mass. If we don't have the axis of rotation on the center of the puzzle, we very well may not see the picture."

It took us another thirty minutes of using the scissors and carefully experimenting with taking off small bits of cardboard before we had everything ready to try.

I smiled at Emily, "Here we go," I said as I gently tossed the replica into the air.

"Nothing," Emily said when I looked her way. "The lines all blurred together, and made a series of circles."

"You mean concentric circles?"

"I don't know if that's what they are called. A bunch of circles that all have the same center."

"Yep, those would be concentric." I ran my fingers through my hair. "Why didn't we see something," I grumbled. "I really thought that we would see something when we spun it."

"Tell me again about what Einstein did and why you thought this would work."

"Emily!"

"No, Stevie, I'm serious. Maybe by explaining it to me, again, it'll trigger something so that we remember what we forgot."

"Okay, I can see that." I spent the next five minutes going over the experiment that I had read about.

"Something important has been overlooked, Stevie. That's all."

"Yeah, that's all. It's only something important, and I can't figure out what it was, or is."

"Okay, then let's talk about something else for a few minutes and we can come back to this. So what is this supposed to do?" she asked as she waved her fingers in front of her face.

"It causes a strobing effect," I answered. "It momentarily blocks the light which causes…" I paused, and thought for a moment. "I wonder. What if we need to strobe this?"

"Strobe what?" she asked.

I was beyond the point of answering questions, or thinking of anything beyond how to strobe the puzzle. I dashed to Kyle's room and out of habit knocked before I went in. I wasn't supposed to go in to his room, especially if he wasn't there, but right now I needed something that he had: a camera flash.

Kyle had gotten interested in photography when he was still in middle school. Over the past few years, his interest had expanded and my grandparents had slowly purchased the parts for a very nice camera system for him.

I went over to his Tamarack bag and opened it carefully. If anything happened to any of his equipment, I would be in big trouble. I found his flash unit, and ran back downstairs.

As an afterthought, I texted him asking where he was and if I could borrow the flash. He responded back almost immediately saying I could as long as I was careful. I grinned at Emily, "I probably should have done that first, but hey, I'm legal now."

"I've always gone with the idea that it's better to ask forgiveness than permission."

I turned out the lights in the family room, set the pulse on the flash unit and gave the disc a spin.

"Do you see that?" I asked Emily, in an awed voice.

CHAPTER 10:

HIDDEN MESSAGES

Opening the door, Mom came into the room slowly. "May I inquire as to why all of the lights are off?"

"Hi, Mom. I had an idea that I needed to run with for solving the clue. Watch." I set the flash to strobe and sent the puzzle-disk spinning.

"There's something written on there, isn't there?" Mom asked in a surprised tone.

"Yeah. While we were at the mall, they have that fountain by the food court, you know? Anyway, while I was waiting for Emily to get her lunch, I was looking at the fountain and I thought of Albert Einstein. It was only a short hop from there to the idea that what we were seeing was a still picture of an object in motion."

Mom had sat down on the edge of the sofa, and was looking at me as if I'd just landed on my head.

"You can't deny what you just saw, Mom. I think we've got the first part of the clue under control."

"Well, I suppose that is excellent considering that it is April. But I think for now, we need to put this away, so we can get to your grandparents' for dinner.

We left a few minutes after Emily, and Mom turned the conversation to some topics that had been discussed at my grandparents' house during the afternoon. My mind however was still tuned in on trying to figure out the clue. I was close, but it was still just out of reach.

Deciding that I wanted to spend some extra time with Aunt Nancy before Easter, I opted to work in the kitchen making a variety of goodies. My mom came down and found me sitting at the breakfast bar, wearing a pair of old sweats along with my favorite sweatshirt, having a cup of tea.

"Do I assume, by the way that you are dressed, that I am going to be having company today making cookies and pies?"

"Yeah. I heard you and Aunt Nancy talking about doing this, and thought it would be good for me to refresh my memory on how it's done. I don't think I've wanted to make a pie since I was in maybe fourth grade. I guess it's time, huh?"

Mom just laughed. "It's always time to make sweets, but you're right. It's always a nice time when you get a couple of hours to spend with each other."

Nancy rolled in, "Did I hear someone mention that we've got a slave today?" she asked giving me a wink.

"Stevie decided that she wants to help with the baking."

Trying to fit myself into the production scheme that Mom and Nancy had, was a challenge. Not only did I have to keep track of the amounts that were going in and the time, I had to ensure that things didn't block any of the paths. It was while we were all taking a short break that I decided to ask them both what they thought about any ideas of how to break this code.

"It's frustrating," I said. "I know that there is something written there, but I can't get enough of a spin to see it fully."

Nancy stared into her coffee. "It seems to me that what you need to do is find a method that would spin the puzzle at a specific speed for a longer period of time."

"But she'd have to find one that she could match with the strobe," Mom added.

"Maybe I should run back out to the mall," I noted. "They have one of those shops where they sell all sorts or wacky things. I remember when I was there yesterday, that they had a strobe light for sale in the main display window."

In the end, we decided that I'd just use Kyle's flash for now and I had a few ideas of how to get the disk spinning. The best probably came from my dad who suggested that we mount it on a variable speed drill and video everything. Now all I had to do was get the time to get out to the shop to try it.

Rushing to the shop that night after dinner was over, I hoped that I'd find a little time that I could work on the clue. Dad had helped me set up the flash unit along with a stand for a video camera so that we could record all of the trials.

I literally held my breath the first time that I pulled the trigger on the drill, afraid that the cardboard would totally come apart and everything would be set back. But, everything seemed to work okay. I had to remember to close my eyes so that I wouldn't be blinded by the constant flashing light.

I tried several variations, each time changing only one variable, usually the speed of the strobe. It took a while before I began to get anywhere. Unfortunately, by the time I was getting close, it was pushing midnight and I was too cold and tired to continue.

Lying in my bed, I reviewed what I'd seen on the video. I was getting close to having everything in sync. I could see words start and then rotate out of focus, and then emerge again. It was a case where I needed to fine-tune the timing between the disk and the strobe light.

But even with as little as was visible now, I was sure that the actual clue wasn't in English. I was hoping that it would end up in a language either I, or one of my close friends, knew. I thought back to the last clue; the one where the only word on it had been in Dutch that had then been written in Greek letters.

Crawling out of bed, I went over to my desk and took the box that held the three medallions. Clearing a spot on my desk, I laid all three of the medallions out in the order in which I found them. There was nothing that stood out about any of them, or that looked unusual. I decided that it must just be the fact that May was literally around the corner, and my mind was starting to get antsy about everything.

I reached over to turn out the light when the shadow of my arm fell across one of the medals. "What's this?" I asked aloud. I looked closer at the very bottom of the medal there was definitely something there. I went back and looked at the other two as well. There were similar markings on each. Not exactly the same, but similar. It almost looked like the patterns would match up, but the light wasn't good enough to make any progress.

I looked at Misty, "We'll figure it out in the morning," I promised her as I turned out the night and drifted off to sleep.

Using a bright LED light in the morning, I studied the markings on the three medallions out in my shop. I had them spread out on the main table, and was now moving them around trying to see if I could get the patterns to match. "Come in," I yelled to the knock on the door.

"You look pretty busy here," Ian said as he walked though the door.

I went over to where he stood shaking off his coat to give him a proper welcome. "It's been kind of dull around here without you."

"Well, we all had to go down to my great-aunt's place. My mom decided that we should take a few extra days there. Can't say that I'm really sorry to be back, though." He smiled and grabbed me around the waist and crushed me to him.

This is what I'd been missing subconsciously over the last few days. My life had been active, but here was someone who understood me better than almost anyone.

"So," he asked when he let go, "what are you working on?"

"I've got several things going on right now. I think the clue on the puzzle is a stop motion picture," I said pointing to the drill set-up. "I'm going to try to fine tune it today and see if I can't get the words to pop out. But the thing that I'm working on right now is trying to see if I can make out these small symbols on the bottoms of the medallions."

I handed Ian one of the medals. He rubbed his finger over the bottom and changed the angle that he was holding it at. "Hmmm. I can see something there. It's almost like a watermark or something. It's not real clear, but it is there."

"Like I said, I found them on all three of the medallions. I figure that they must be important for something."

"I've got an idea that may or may not work. Interested?"

"Let's hear it."

"We'll wash them and then use a cloth to pat dry. I've got a black light at home that I can go get and we'll try that."

"Okay, but I'm a little confused on what this is going to do."

"Many detergents have phosphorus in them to make your whites brighter. The phosphorus will glow under a black light."

An hour later we were standing around looking at the symbols that were now fluorescing. "Obviously, they go together," I said. "Look how these parts on the first match up with the ones on this part on the second."

"I think you're right, Stevie, which means that it is very likely that the third medal fits here between the two." He dropped it into place, "Bingo! Now all we need to do is figure out what it all means."

"I'm going to use the camera and grab a few photos of this so that was can look at it with the lights on." Leaving the camera on the tripod, I took several shots varying the shutter speed, hoping that something would be useful.

I took twelve shots before I got a few that I felt would give us what we were looking for. "You know what? I've got a bad feeling about this."

"About what?" Ian asked.

"It seems that whenever we have to solve a clue or a puzzle, there is a task that I have to do as well."

"Well, lets see if we can figure it out. But before we spend too much time on this, let's see if we can get the other clue to photograph as well. Then we can get us all together to see what the group of us can do."

On the fourth try, we hit the jackpot; the words became visible and remained constant enough that we thought we could possibly read them. "Darn! It is in a different language," I complained. "I was hoping that it wouldn't be."

Ian laughed, "It's always nice to hope. At least it appears to be in Latin again. That simplifies things a bit."

"For you, sure. For those of us who don't know Latin, it doesn't help anything."

I checked the digital shots that we had taken along with the videos. Everything looked good. "Let's pack all of this in and make some calls. Maybe we can even convince Mom to make some cookies for our little pow-wow.

Together, we packed up all of the materials and headed to the house, hand-in-hand.

Mom did have cookies ready; kiss cookies, which she made me share with everyone. But that was okay. Nonni, Poppy, Kyle, Mom and Dad sat dispersed on the furniture in the family room, while Chrissy, Emily, Ian and I took up seats on the floor. Aunt Nancy had positioned herself near the coffee table, or more to the point, near the cookies.

Kyle had helped me hook the cameras up to the television, and now we all were looking at the two different clues that we had found today.

"Any idea what that phrase means?" I asked Ian as I pointed to the phrase currently on the screen.

"*Pietas est cor proprio invoca. Amicus, omnium misereatur*, as best as I can tell means, 'Compassion is the heart's own call. Be a friend, have compassion for all'."

"In a strange way, that almost makes sense," Aunt Nancy pointed out.

We all looked at her. "Could you elaborate on that?" I asked.

"Sure," she said. "In the first task, you had to learn about honesty. Task two was loyalty. Each of these are tenets of what most people would consider required to make up a decent society. Following that idea, the idea of compassion would make sense."

I sat for a minute; what she said made sense, but I was unsure if this was the connection between all three or not. "Okay, I guess I could buy that. Any body have any ideas on what the other symbols mean?"

CHAPTER 11:

EYE OPENERS

School was back in session the following week. The first day back was one of those days where nothing seemed to fit right. I'd made it through the morning classes without too much trouble, but when I went to my English class after lunch things fell apart.

"Stevie," Ms. Daily called me. She motioned to the hall, "May I speak with you out here, please?"

I took a deep breath. As far as I knew everything that was due was already handed in. Although, I decided that there was the possibility that with everything that had been going on with the clue and the curse, that I might have overlooked something.

"What's up, Ms. Daily?" I asked tentatively.

"Stevie, I was going through the papers that were turned in just before vacation. When I got to yours, it sounded familiar. A little too familiar, actually. As I sat there wondering why it did, it was because I'd just read the same paper minutes before. Only this one had Tanya Spitz's name on it. I'd like to know why you decided to cheat?"

"How did Tanya get my paper?" I blurted out. "Ms. Daily, you helped me re-write sections of that paper. You know that I didn't cheat." Tears were now streaming down my face.

"Stevie, I have no choice in this. I gave both papers to Mrs. Lerch this morning, and asked to speak to the students involved first. The school policy on this is that both students receive a grade of zero for that assignment. I'm sorry about that, but unless it can be proven that you had no part in this, that is the way it has to be."

She turned and went back into the classroom, leaving me crying silently by the bank of lockers.

I let myself slide down the cold steel of the lockers, and sat hunched on the floor. "Looks like it must have been pretty devastating news," Ian's voice said from somewhere nearby.

"I didn't know that you were here. Shouldn't you be in class?"

He knelt down, "I could ask the same, but I know that this is where you are supposed to be. Want to tell me what's got you out here crying? Once you let me know who hurt you, I can go beat them up," he said with a smile.

"It's Tanya Spitz. Somehow she got a copy of my English paper, and copied it and turned it in. Mrs. Daily recognized that the two papers were the same. Now we both get zeros. For her, she probably doesn't care. But for me? This is devastating."

He sat down next to me and draped his arm around me. "Let's hold off on beating any body up. I think I know how we might be able to solve this, where you can get the grade that you earned, and she'll get what she deserves."

"How, Ian? This stands unless I can prove that I wasn't involved with this in any way. It's basically my words against hers."

"Let's get to our classes, and we'll think about this a bit later. Relax," he said giving me a light kiss. "I've got a few ideas. This will work out in the end." He rubbed my shoulders and strode away.

I took a deep breath to steady myself and went in to join my class. Thankfully, no one asked, so I was able to get through the rest of the class by simply going through the motions.

Emily caught up with me after class. I was walking in a daze down the hall towards History. "Hey, Stevie! Why didn't you wait for me?"

I kept walking, totally caught in my own little world that was crashing down around me. Somewhere in the middle of English, I realized that I had to let my folks know about this. I was pretty sure that they weren't going to be happy with the news.

A hand grabbed my shoulder and tugged, "Stevie! What's going on? You look like..." She paused. "Stevie? You in there?" She snapped her fingers in front of my eyes.

"Huh?" I blinked, and then focused on Emily. "Oh, God, Em. What am I going to do?" I cried.

She stared at me totally clueless as to what had brought on the water works. "You want to try stating at the beginning? Maybe if I understood the whole problem, I'd be able to give some advice."

I laughed lightly, "I'm sorry." We walked to History, me leaning on her and telling her the story.

Nudging me as we came up to the classroom, Emily pointed with her chin, "Well, speak of the devil."

I looked towards the doorway, and saw Gabby and Tanya standing just outside. "Hmm, looks like they're having an argument of some kind. Too bad we can't hear what's going on." We watched for a few seconds more. "Hey, Em? Is it me or does Gabby really look like she's not well? I mean, she's pale, and it looks like she's got dark circles under her eyes."

"I think that she probably didn't put her makeup on this morning before she went to court."

"I'd forgotten that she had that today. Well, we can most probably assume that since she is here, that she didn't get time in jail."

"That's too bad. After they way she's treated you and Chrissy and a whole bunch of other people, I wouldn't mind seeing her shoved off to a cell for a while. She might learn something from it."

"Emily, we can't think like that. That would just bring us down to her level. I'm going to hope that she already has learned something from this."

The bell rang, so we ran the last ten feet to the door and ducked in just as Mrs. Vallente was coming to close it.

Gabby and Tanya came through the door as Emily and I were taking our seats. I looked at the two of them. Tanya, strutting with her bleached blonde hair wearing shorts and flip-flops. Gabby was a step behind and was dressed in a nice blouse and slacks, no doubt what she'd worn to court that morning. But it was the way that Gabby carried herself that caught my attention.

She didn't have her head up in that usual pompous fashion. She was looking down at the floor, and her right arm seemed to cradle her stomach.

"Em," I whispered, "did you see the way Gabby was cradling her stomach?"

"My guess is lunch didn't sit well. I don't feel so good either. Let it go, Stevie."

I didn't really want to let it go. Aside from the clues for the curse, it was the only thing that I had that I could ponder on, while trying to look attentive during class.

Watching Gabby through class, I tried to look at her face to see if she was showing any signs of pain. She showed no signs that I could see. But her arms often cradled her stomach. I wondered to myself if perhaps I was seeing things, or if Gabby was by chance pregnant.

When Mrs. Valletne ended class and gave us time to work on our assignment, I took the chance and leaned over to Emily. "Psst, Em?"

"What?" she whispered back.

"I think maybe I'm going crazy. But I've been watching Gabby all class. She's been cradling her stomach the whole time. I wonder if she's, you know…"

"You think that maybe she's been knocked up?" Emily's voice was louder than I would have liked, but still not loud enough to be heard over the other voices.

I just raised my eyebrows in answer. "That might explain the secretive stuff, her being by herself and all. I don't know, but it is something that I may need to talk to Ian about."

"Why? If she's gotten in trouble, that's her deal, not yours. Why are you so concerned with her right now, anyway?"

"I don't know. It's like when I see her, I feel that what she needs right now, more than anything, is a real friend."

"She's got Tanya. Problem solved."

"I'm not sure she does."

After school, I took the bus home since I wanted to be able to say good-bye to Aunt Nancy, who would be heading to the airport shortly after four. Bursting through the door, I rounded into the kitchen where I expected to find Mom and Aunt Nancy there with a plate of cookies. Instead, I found Kyle and two of his friends, and an empty plate.

"Did you even leave me one?" I asked Kyle.

"There should be a few in the freezer. Sorry. Well, not really. They were very good." He laughed as he and his friends headed outside with their mitts to play catch.

Grumbling, I went to the freezer, opened the bag of cookies and took only what I needed. As I headed for the stairs, I tripped over Misty and dropped two of my little treasures. The quick little dog grabbed one of the frozen treats and dashed up the stairs.

I stopped to retrieve the second cookie. Heading for my room once more, I turned to find my mom standing there, her hands on her hips. "Stevie, would you care to explain why you're stealing cookies from the freezer? And then, even worse, why you'd give one to your dog?"

I burst into tears, again. "Kyle and his fr-fr-friends ate all the co-cookies that were out. I-I wanted a snack, so I grabbed some from the freezer. Then I tripped and Misty ran off with one before I could get it from her. It's been a horrible day."

I felt her arms come around me, "Okay, let's go in the family room and talk about it."

Watching Dad pull out of the driveway with Aunt Nancy an hour later made me melancholy. I loved her so much; she was my favorite aunt, but she lived so far away that I hardly got to see her. So, I stood there in the doorway watching the car go down the street and wondered when I'd get to see her again.

My phone rang interrupting my thoughts, "Hello?" I answered.

"Stevie, it's Ian." His voice was rough, almost like he was fighting back tears.

"Ian, what's wrong?"

"I don't want to get into it over the phone. Would there be any chance that we could get together for a little while this evening?"

"Do you want to come over here?"

"How about I pick you up, and then we can go somewhere some-what private for dinner?"

"Okay. That should work. What time?"

"Let's plan for around seven. That should give me enough time for everything that I need to do first."

"Ian, are you in some kind of trouble? What can I do to help?"

"Right now, there's nothing that you can do, Stevie. Thanks for asking, but there isn't anything that anyone can do."

"Ian, you're scaring me."

"Stevie, right now, just knowing that I'm going to be with you later this evening is going to give me the strength to get through what I've got to do. I love you. I've gotta go. See you around seven." The line clicked dead.

I stared at my phone. This day had been rough going from the start, why should it get better now?

Standing in the doorway, I looked over at my Mom who was now busy at the stove. "What's up, Honey?" she asked.

"I'm not really sure. Ian just called, he sounded a bit distraught; he said he needed to talk to me later tonight. He's picking me up around seven."

"Are things okay between you two?"

"If you'd asked me that ten minutes ago, I would have said yes without hesitation. After hearing him on the phone, I'm insecure enough to wonder." I wandered into the kitchen and grabbed a Coke out of the refrigerator. Popping the top, I leaned back on the counter and stared at the windows on the other side.

Mom walked over, wiped her hands on the towel that she was carrying, and draped her arm around my shoulders. "Stevie, regardless of what happens, remember that we are all here for you."

"I know. It's just hard to think that things may be falling apart on me now. It's the first time that I've ever had a boyfriend, I've made significant strides at school taking on leadership roles and, even if I must say so myself, I've managed to handle all of this curse stuff fairly well."

"That you have, honey. Trust me, everything will be okay." She kissed the top of my head and went back to working on dinner.

After a minute, I called out to her, "Mom, I'm heading out to the shop for a little while."

Entering the shop, I stood quietly in the door studying the room. So much of my life of the past two years had been spent out here. Alone. Now that Ian was in the picture, the future that I'd originally planned for myself had changed slightly.

As I picked up the wrench from the table and began to install some of the lines for the engine, I wondered if the changes I now saw were in response to my relationship with Ian or because of how I had grown this year from everything else.

The longer I worked, the more I realized that the answer was yes on both counts. It brought back the discussion that Aunt Nancy and I had had right here in the shop. Things that happened in our lives were like puzzle pieces. Right now, I was looking carefully at the pieces of my puzzle. There were certain things that I realized that I would let go if need be. Things that I had once thought of as "too important" had now been relegated to the point that I could live without them.

What it all meant was that I needed to decide what was important enough to fight for, and how much I would be willing to concede to win those points.

For the better part of an hour, I worked and thought with only the radio playing providing any distraction. When I set the tools down, and stood back I smiled. My little Sonex project was almost ready to become a full-fledged airplane.

She stood proudly on her main gear, the new engine was now totally installed with all lines run and ready to fill with oil and gas. Her wings, currently hung from the rafters, were ready to be mounted and stretched. She was ready to reach out to find her true potential.

I realized as I looked at her, that she was the aluminum embodiment of me. I stood here, nearly a high school graduate, ready to stretch my own wings and try flying on my own.

The swell of pride that I felt at this exact moment was stupendous. I stood, mesmerized by the complex feelings and embraced it.

The first part of my flight tonight, was that I was going to do what ever it took to keep Ian and I together.

The alarm on my phone rang. A look at the screen and I took a deep breath and said to the empty shop, "Show time."

CHAPTER 12:

STRANGE BREW

Downtown Scarborough was flashing by the car windows as I stared out. The ride from home had been eerily silent, and Ian was looking ahead about as stoically as a martyr. I kept reminding myself that I would assert myself and I would get what I what I wanted tonight. "Where are we going tonight?" I asked primarily as a diversion from the silence.

"I'm sorry, Stevie. I'm not very good company tonight. I thought that going somewhere out of town might be a nice break for both of us. There's a little diner in the older section of Scarborough. We'll be there in a couple of minutes. Tiny's is a small family owned place, that actually has atmosphere and privacy."

Oh-oh, I thought. He's after privacy. That surely doesn't bode well for us. Better to be prepared for whatever came my way.

He turned into the small parking lot and pulled in to a space near the front. I could see the awning that hung over the doorway. A red neon sign proclaimed that this was Tiny's and various others advertised what beverages they had on tap.

I lingered for a moment, using the mirror on the sun visor to apply some lip-gloss. Ian hadn't said what the dress code was for tonight, so I'd gone with casual. As usual, I'd neglected to put any makeup on before leaving home. I hoped the lip-gloss made me look like I belonged here.

Ian held the door for me and then took my hand. As we walked, he squeezed my hand several times. It was almost as if he was gathering strength from me.

Inside Tiny's, antique plaques and advertisements hung along the walls. A display case in the waiting area had a collection of political campaign buttons that must have ranged from the last fifty years.

A middle-aged woman stepped out from the door on the side. She was pleasantly plump as my mom would have called her, and had her light brown hair set in a shoulder length bob. "Hi, welcome to Tiny's. Just the two of you?"

Ian nodded, "We have a reservation, under Morris."

She consulted her book, "Yes, you do. Please follow me." She led us through the main portion of the restaurant where framed art hung on the walls illuminated by individual track lights. We passed several small round tables covered with checkerboard tablecloths and then turned and headed out to what appeared to be a covered porch.

Lattice hung from the rafters, with fake vines and grape bunches tacked on. Small white lights added to the ambiance as she led us out to one of the two tables that were placed here.

Setting the menus on the table, she turned, "Lucy will be your server tonight, and she'll be right out to get your drink orders. Enjoy your meal."

"This is nice," I said as I took the seat that Ian held for me.

Ian took the seat across from me just as Lucy appeared. She quickly took our drink and appetizer order and headed back to the kitchen. "Ian, can you tell me what's going on right now? You look concerned about something, which you so rarely are." I reached across the table and took his hand. I figured if he was going to try breaking up with me, he was at least going to have to have a bit of physical contact to get through.

His reaction surprised me. He didn't try to pull away; instead he squeezed my hand tighter. It only made the whole scenario that much more awkward. I could tell that there was something very important that he wanted to tell me. He started to speak, and fumbled his words. "Stevie, I, we, um. Oh, blast it all!'

"It's okay, Ian. Take a breath, let it out slowly and tell me what's on your mind."

Tears suddenly rolled down his cheeks. Now I was nervous. "Ian, what is it?"

He looked at me and stuttered, "There's a whole heap of things that are bearing down on me right now." He used the napkin to wipe his eyes dry. "You asked me the other day if I knew what was going on with Gabby. Well, I finally asked my mom tonight after school. She'd been crying as well, so that set me off."

He paused while Lucy delivered our drinks and took our order for a pizza. Once she had gone, he continued.

"When I got home today, my mom was sitting on the couch clutching her arms around her, crying and rocking back and forth. At first, I thought that perhaps my Grandma had passed away. When I asked her, she shook her head and only mouthed Annie."

Annie was Gabby's mom. I didn't know her well, as I had only met her a few times. Ian had said that she had been going for tests. "Did they find something in the testing?"

Ian nodded his head. "Annie and my mom have been like sisters since they were in grade school. When Annie and my uncle started going out, my mom was ecstatic. She was over the moon when they got married, and they've stayed close. Over the years, I would say that Aunt Annie has been my favorite aunt, even if her daughter is a few steps out of kilter."

I smiled lightly when he referenced Gabby. But then my thoughts turned back to what he had looked like moments before. "So, what happened today?" I asked prompting him back to the story.

He stared at something that was over my shoulder. His eyes were glistening again as he fought for control. "Apparently Aunt Annie called my mom this afternoon, right before I came in from school. They've diagnosed her as having uterine cancer."

"Oh, Ian. I'm so sorry."

"Nobody has said whether or not they think that they've caught it early enough for the treatments to be effective. But they're all trying to be positive."

I thought about how I would feel if I'd received news like this about Aunt Nancy. I was pretty sure that my world would implode. I'd probably lock myself in my room and wallow in self-pity until I was forcibly dragged out.

Yet, Ian hadn't done that. Instead, he'd called me and asked me to go out somewhere somewhat private while he worked through his anger and concerns. The fears that I'd worked myself up to in the shop earlier became silly. He'd asked me to be with him because he needed me to help get him through this.

I slid my chair over so I was closer to him, and drew him into my arms, letting his head rest on my shoulders. My hands traced out small circles on his back. "I'm here for you, Ian. We have to believe that she'll get through this."

"Stevie, this is only part of what's been weighing on Gabby. I know that you don't see eye-to-eye with her, but to find out that one of your parents is that sick, would put a major weight on your shoulders. To top if off, her dad has been having some issues at work. It seems that nearly a quarter of a million dollars has gone missing from the company. No one is talking about it right now, but it seems that someone that my Uncle David hired, embezzled the money. Of course, since it went on for so long, his job is now in jeopardy."

He looked up. "Couple those things together, and she's dealing with a lot of nastiness on her plate right now. From what I've seen, and my mom reiterated from her talks with Annie,

Gabby's friends have distanced themselves from her due to the whole legal mess."

"That had to be about the ultimate topper," I said. "Your mom ends up sick, your dad may lose his job, and you're going to court because you did something foolish. Even if you end up getting off lightly in court, you are going to be ridiculed by the others in the school because your actions have consequences for them as well."

"You hit it pretty much on the head. From what Aunt Annie relayed, Gabby ended up on probation for six months, but some of the others are looking at actual jail terms. Gabby's been seeing a therapist trying to work through things, but still it's a lot to deal with."

Lucy came with our pizza then. "Here you two go," she said as she served. "Be careful, it's hot." She took the empty glasses and returned back to the kitchen.

"Ian, do you talk at all with Gabby?"

"Huh? What do you mean?"

"I mean, I've noticed her on a few occasions, and have even tried to talk to her a few times in the past week or so. Maybe you could let her know that if she'd like to talk, I'd be willing to put our past behind us and be there to listen to her."

"Your offer surprises me, Stevie. But I'll pass it on."

"It gives her a choice, that's all. Right now, if I was in her shoes, and the people that I thought were my friends were abandoning me, I'd be thankful for someone who would be willing to help."

"You're not going to reciprocate to what she did that one day last March, are you?"

"You mean drug her and get her to spill her deepest secrets? No. I've had that done to me, and it only hurts you more. Gabby's actually trying to do the right thing with Chrissy's situation, and it's costing her more than I think anyone else knows."

"Like I said, I'll pass it on to her."

We finished the pizza while talking about other things that were going on at school. Finally, we moved to the topic of the clue.

"I'm still not sure what to make of the symbols that we found in the center of the three medallions."

"I can understand that," Ian said. "The weird thing about them is that I would almost swear that I've seen that symbol before."

My curiosity peaked. "Where do you think you've seen it before? I mean, when we had the last symbol on the last clue, it ended up being on the headstone in the cemetery. So, if you've got any ideas, I'd love to hear them."

"I actually wondered if I'd seen it there. I went back there the other day, while you were out with Emily at the mall. I kept looking around hoping that I'd see it and be able to give you some help with that end of things. No luck though."

"It was worth a shot. Thanks for looking." I sipped at the Coke that was on the table. "I just wish that something would click into place. The whole part about having compassion is in some ways too simple but in other ways too cryptic to be certain of what it means."

"I was wondering, is that the only reason that you extended the offer to Gabby? Trying to break the curse?"

"No!" I was mortified that he could even think that. "Ian, it's just that I've been there. For most of my academic career, I've been the one left standing on the sidelines. The one who never had the support of my classmates. I know how it is. Finding out what she is dealing with right now, I don't know. I can't say as I'd wish it on anyone. But right now, she needs someone who will be there to help her pick up the pieces of her life and get everything back on track."

Lucy returned to clear our table and get our desert order. "Might I recommend the chocolate-peanut butter pie? It's one of our specialties."

I looked at Ian. He knew my weakness for that particular combination. "That sounds perfect. We'll do two, and I'll have a cup of coffee," he said.

"Tea for me, please," I requested. She left and we were alone again for a few minutes.

"Ian," I asked tentatively. "Did your mom say what your aunt's prognosis was?"

He shook his head. "I know that Annie is going to see the oncologist on Wednesday, and that she will be starting treatments as soon as possible. Hopefully, everything will work out."

I reached out and took his hand, gave it a squeeze. "It'll be okay. That's what you keep telling me, right? Well, now it's my turn." I smiled at him and gave a wink as Lucy returned with two plates heaped with mounds of chocolate.

Glancing up at the stars that now filled the clear night sky, I leaned on Ian's shoulder as we walked hand in hand from the restaurant to his car. "Thank you," I said. "Thank you for dinner, and for trusting me to be there for you."

He turned me, and looking me in my eyes said, "Stevie, you're the only person that I could trust with this. My mom is too close, and she is trying to get through this as well. The whole thing is too close to reminding us how my dad died."

I hadn't thought of that one. It was another reasons that this was hitting him so hard. "Sorry, I'd forgot about that," I admitted.

"Not your fault. Just brings back memories that I'd prefer to forget. But we'll deal with what is, as opposed to what we'd wish for."

The trip home was short, but my mind was spinning as I thought of what had transpired this evening. When I'd left the house, three hours before, I was afraid that Ian was planning to end our relationship. It turned out he needed me more now than before. It put me in an interesting situation; trying to be there to comfort and console him as his aunt goes through her treatments, but also trying to figure out how to solve the clue that holds the key to my future.

I looked up again at the clear sky. May was around the corner, and I had very little to go on right now, but the stakes were much higher. Everything seemed to hinge on a symbol that looked familiar, but no one seemed to know from where.

I'm sure that it was only in my mind, but I would have sworn that I heard the cackle of the witch, as she celebrated what she was envisioning as my defeat.

It had taken us nearly twelve weeks to figure out the last symbol. I only had six left. Unfortunately, I could do the math a little too easily this time.

CHAPTER 13:

FIELD TRIP

Conflicting schedules between school and other commitments had kept the time that Ian and I had together to a minimum for the last week. May had brought along nice weather, and everyone was trying to get ready for the summer tourist season.

Ian had been helping his mom with her shop, so that she would have the time to go with Annie for her treatments. He was tired most days in school, and I guessed this was due to his working every night until after ten before he could go home and start his homework.

This whole cycle really couldn't have come at a much worse time school wise, as May is when they do the AP exams. So, his work schedule had increased, at the same time he was trying to prepare for these exams. It seemed that every time I saw him, he was pulling his hair out.

Our schedules appeared that they might actually coincide with some free time on Saturday, so we quickly made our plans to spend the day together. "What should we do?" I asked Ian on Thursday. We were talking on our phones after the shop had closed, and he was doing the basic cleanup.

"I don't know. From what I've seen the weather looks like it's supposed to be pretty good. We could actually plan something outdoors and enjoy the sun like normal people."

I laughed. "That would be nice," I agreed. "How about a picnic? We could pack some stuff up, go into the park and just lounge?"

"Hmm, that actually sounds good. What should we pack and when do you want to leave?"

Just as I was about to answer, my phone beeped signaling that I had an incoming call waiting. "Hold on, Ian. My dad is on the other line. Back in a sec." I pressed the button and switched over. "Hi, Dad. What's up?"

"Just wanted to get to you before you made too many plans. Your granddad needs help at the airport over the weekend. I told him that you, Kyle and I would be there first thing Saturday morning."

"Dad!" I protested. "That's the first day that Ian's and my schedules have an opening. He's been working at his mom's shop since his aunt got sick. We'd been planning on going out for a picnic that day."

"Sorry, Stevie. It'll only take the morning. Well, actually it'll probably be closer to three when we finish. We need you there. We'll talk more about this when I get in. I've got to go now. Bye," and he hung up.

I sat there looking at the phone in my hand, quelling the urge to pitch the blasted thing against the wall. I closed my eyes and took a deep breath before pressing the button to return to Ian.

"I wished I hadn't answered that call."

"Bad news, huh?"

"My dad decided that we would all be going to help Poppy at the airport on Saturday. They've got a big breakfast scheduled there next week, and he's got to get everything ready for it."

There was a silence on the other end. "Stevie, I thought your granddad ran an airport, not a restaurant. Why would he be getting ready to serve a breakfast?"

I laughed. "I keep forgetting that not everyone was brought up where fly-in breakfasts were part of the normal every day life. Next week, Poppy's airport will put on a pancake breakfast. The idea is that pilots will fly in for it, it's being advertised locally as well so many families will drive in. The end result will be a community gathering where many people will be exposed to airplanes for the first time. Well, at least, little airplanes. For those that want, there will even be opportunities for them to go flying for a scenic tour of the area."

"Oh. Okay, that makes sense, I guess. What kind of things do you have to do there this weekend?"

"Probably mow the grass, help clean out the main hangar, set up tables. That kind of stuff."

"What if I came to help? Would they let us work together doing some of the chores?"

"They probably would. Thanks, Ian. You've just given me a way that we can all win."

Poppy had dispatched Dad and Kyle to take the tractor and go to the storage hangar on the other side of the airport to pick up a load of tables. Meanwhile, the three of us were moving some projects around in the main hangar to make room for the tables.

"So, what actually goes on in this hangar most of the time?" Ian asked.

"Well," Poppy answered, "we have our maintenance group housed here. So when someone needs a mechanic, this is where they work on the planes. We also rent out some of the space to owners who want to keep their planes out of the elements, but don't want to pay for an entire hangar."

Ian looked over to me. Clearly he was lost as to why someone wouldn't want to pay for the entire hangar. "Some of the planes, like this little Ercoupe would only fill about half of a normal hangar. So they store it here, and save a bit."

"Okay, that makes sense." He asked other questions as the morning wore on, often having a follow up question. It always looked to me that he was filing the information away for use later.

The day went by quickly, and by noon, we had pretty much gotten everything done. Nonni and Mom brought out a plate of sandwiches that we ate at the picnic table just behind the main terminal.

"So what are you kids going to do this afternoon?" Nonni asked.

I shrugged. "We had planned to go out for a picnic today in the park, but plans got changed."

"Scott, did you make her change her plans to come here and help?" Poppy asked.

"Not exactly, Poppy. He just informed me that he had committed me here. Ian decided that we'd work together to at least get a little time."

Poppy looked over at Ian. "I'm thankful for your help, son. I'm also happy to hear that your aunt is responding well to her first round of treatment."

"It was entertaining and educational, so I'm glad I could help. Having Aunt Annie in the hospital has been stressful on everyone. I'm glad as well that she is doing well, and that so many people are supporting her."

I looked up at the sound of an aircraft overhead. I think I may have sighed out loud; it had been a few weeks since I'd managed to get a few hours away to go fly and just let myself go.

"Stevie, I do have one other chore that I need to do today, that I'm hoping that you and Ian can help me with."

Regretfully I let my gaze come down from the plane to his face. "What's that?" I asked trying to put on a good tone.

"The 195 needs to have an oil change. Do you think that you and Ian could take it out for about an hour or so to warm everything up?"

I'm not sure whose mouth was hanging farther open: Ian's or mine.

"I can definitely get into doing that! What do you think, Ian?"

"Um, I'm not sure." When I looked at him, he glanced around nervously. "The truth is, Stevie, I've never been up in anything smaller than a Boeing jet, and I'm afraid of heights," he said softly.

"It's okay, Ian." Oh, I so wanted to go take that flight. But there was no way that I was going to do it without him.

"Ian," Nonni said. "When I first met Bill, I'd never been in a small plane either. But he took me up, and that first flight is one of my best memories. And as for the fear of heights, you'll totally forget about it once you're up." She nodded approvingly.

"Ian," I reached out and took his hand. "If you want, we can give it a try. If you find you don't like it, I can land and we'll make other arrangements."

"I keep forgetting that for you flying is in your blood," Ian said. "Let's give this a try, but go easy on me. No flips or barrel rolls or anything like that."

I laughed. "You really don't want to do anything like that in this plane. It's all going to be straight level flight once we're up. " Turning to Poppy, I bent down and kissed the top of his head. "Thanks, Poppy."

"You're welcome. Just take care of my favorite girl."

"I will," Ian answered.

Poppy roared with laughter. "He's not talking about me," I acknowledged. "He's talking about his plane."

Taking Ian's hand, I led him into the terminal, went into Poppy's office and got the key for the plane. "Ready?"

"I hope so."

"Relax, Ian. This will be a lot of fun." We walked to the hangar nearest the driveway. Unlocking the pass through door, I stepped in and Ian followed. Closing the door, I turned to the large electrical panel on the wall and flipped the switch. With a groan the bi-fold door began to lift and sun peered in through the new opening.

In the streams of sunshine, two silver airplanes sat patiently. The little Cessna140 that I normally flew was nearly dwarfed by the show plane, which had been Poppy's pride and joy for nearly forty years. Her polished aluminum fuselage threw the light rays along the walls like a mirror.

"What kind of plane is this, Stevie?" Ian asked, never taking his eyes off of the plane.

"This is a nineteen-forty-seven Cessna195. This was Poppy's first airplane, and as you can see, he keeps her in show ready condition. I think it's fairly close to original, other than the wings, which are now aluminum."

As I did my pre-flight inspection, I explained everything that I was doing and why it was important that we did that step. When I was done, Ian and I rolled her out onto the apron that surrounded the hangar. Climbing up, we buckled in and I hit the starter button, and the throaty roar of the large radial engine echoed off of the buildings.

Carefully, I finished the before takeoff list, and then eased the throttle forward ever so slightly. The plane taxied slowly, as I used the brakes to maneuver us in an S pattern on the ground.

I saw Ian look at me with a puzzled look on his face. "Since we're in a tail-dragger, visibility over the nose on the ground is not the greatest. By making a series of small turns, I can be sure that we don't hit anything."

As we approached the end of the runway, I made a final radio call, advanced the throttle and straightened out on the centerline. The 195's big prop caught the air and in moments, we were air born.

Climbing to altitude, I continued to explain everything to Ian as a way to help him stay relaxed. A minute later, it became apparent that I didn't need to.

"Oh, my. Stevie, look at that," he said pointing to the horizon. I just smiled. For the next ten minutes he was too occupied with the view out of the window for anything else.

"Want to try something?" I asked.

"What?"

"I want to show you this first. Put your hands on your lap and move your feet back from the pedals." He did, and I showed him that I had done the same. "See, the plane knows how to fly, all by itself. We're just here to give it a little direction. Go ahead and put your hand on the yoke."

"Stevie, do you think this is a good idea? I don't want to break anything."

"Ian, relax. Just give the plane little inputs." He did, and the size of his smile grew as the plane dipped a wing and headed in the new direction that he had chosen.

We spent the next twenty minutes with Ian turning left, right, climbing and descending. Most importantly, he was laughing. "This is so awesome," he said. I'm going to have to learn how to do this."

"I'm sure Poppy can work something out so you can," I said, happy that he was enjoying himself. Something off in the distance caught my eye. "Hey, Ian. Look off the right wing. Do you see that shape in the clearing?"

"Yeah. Think it's some kind of crop circle?"

"I don't know. Let's go take a closer look." I took control of the plane and headed there.

We circled over the clearing in the woods and examined the shape. It appeared to have been defined by large rocks that had been set into the side of the hill. There were several tall rock piles that were spaced in uneven piles randomly around the clearing. Grass of a dark green stood out in the center of the clearing. "It looks familiar to me," Ian said.

"Unless I'm mistaken, that's the same symbol that is in the center of the medallion. And is it me, or do the rock piles look similar to the pattern that appears when the three medals are put together?" I circled around so we could get another look.

Ian looked at me and then out the window again. "I think you may be right.

Overflying the pattern again, I used my hand-held GPS unit to get an exact location of where we were. "We can translate these coordinates onto a map when we get home. Maybe there is some significance to this place."

"At this point, anything is plausible," he responded.

We flew over the area several times, from as many directions as we could. Ian took pictures using his phone so we would have some proof of what we saw. "I wish I had some idea what this was a figure of. It would make things so much easier."

"Solving this clue isn't going to be easy, Stevie. We knew that going in. We're going to be working our butts off to get to the bottom of this."

"I know," I sighed. "But it sure would be nice to have a better handle on it, though."

I glanced at my watch; "It's time to head back to the airport."

"That's a bummer. I really enjoyed this, Stevie. This is something that I may never have done without you. Definitely have to thank your grandmother. I would have likely begged off of this if she hadn't talked to me."

"I'm glad that you didn't. I really love coming up here to let my mind wander and get away from everything that's going on in real life. It's a different world."

"Will that plane you're building in the shop be anything like this one?"

"In some ways. My Sonex is a lot smaller, but it will be less expensive to own and operate. It should be fun to fly, like this one is, and it will be able to do cross-country flights. In general, it'll be a great little plane to have fun with and go to some easy to get to places. But, it's not going to be set up for any kind of instrument flying. So, it's only going to be used to go flying on nice clear days."

"Works for me," he said.

After we landed and put the plane back in the hangar, Ian went to talk to Nonni and Poppy about his experience. I called Poppy's mechanic, Tom, to let him know that the 195 was ready for it's oil change. While I waited, I used the special rag that Poppy kept in the hangar to wipe down the plane.

My mind wandered as I methodically wiped the oil from the plane's belly. What was the figure that we had seen? How did it factor into the clue that I was trying to solve. Why was it etched onto the side of the hill?

It seemed that the closer I got to unraveling one part of the clue, the more twisted and knotted other aspects became. Just my luck, I suppose.

CHAPTER 14:

REVELATIONS

Dressed in my pajamas that night, I sat at the computer playing with the photos that Ian and I had taken during our flight. My original thought was to compile a slide show for Ian, so that he could remember his first flight in a small airplane. I was studying one of the pictures I had taken while he was at the controls; his face lit up like a kid on Christmas. It made him look even younger than he normally does.

I kept adding new shots into the slide show, and then trying to find suitable music that I could add as background. Letting the images and the sounds envelope me, I found my mind wandering back to the flight and remembering my own feelings.

Something from the flight kept trying to edge its way into my consciousness, but I couldn't put my finger on it. I turned to look out the window and the stars beyond, hoping that they might provide the key to what was trying to come forwards.

The next picture that I uploaded was the one of the rock formation that we had seen. I stopped. This was it, the part that I was subconsciously thinking about.

Getting up, I crossed to my desk and retrieved the medallions. Placing the three together like we had earlier, the images were again visible. I remembered that we had taken a picture of this when Ian and I were out in the shop one day.

Grabbing my camera from its case, I uploaded the pictures to the laptop. Finding the right file, I extracted the picture of the glowing medallions that we had done using Ian's black light. Because we had soaked the medallions first in a mixture of water and laundry detergent, they fluoresced when exposed to the black light.

The photo clearly showed the lines of the barely visible images that were inscribed onto the bottoms of the medallions. I manipulated the two photos: the actual medallions and the one from the flight. It took about twenty minutes, but I was finally able to get them to the same orientation and scale.

Using the computer program, I made a copy of each and pasted them into a text document one at a time. Carefully, I changed the opacity of the flight photo, and dragged it so that it lay over the medallion photo. The lines for both matched perfectly. Those rocks that we saw were definitely not some fluke. There was a reason that they were there, just like there was a reason they were on the medallions.

I needed to find out why.

Going to my closet, I pulled down my flight bag to get out my hand held GPS unit. Running through our flight track on screen, I was able to determine the approximate location and size of the rocks. The first question that I had, was why were those rocks there? I had a feeling that there would be some direct link to either my relatives or to Ichabod Crane.

I dialed Ian while I was starting the computer search. "Ian, it's me," I said as soon as he answered. "I was going through the photos form the flight, and something caught my eye." I explained about how the two images fit together. "No, I don't mean that they kind of look alike, I mean that they are exact."

"How can they be exact?" he wanted to know.

"When I made them the same scale, and placed them together everything lines up. These images are not just made to look like each other, the points and characteristics are the same on each. They were deliberately made to be exact replicas of each other."

"Don't you think you're reading too much into this, Stevie?"

"No. Seriously, what are the odds that we would find two random symbols that share the same shape have exactly the same ratios for all parts concerned and not be somehow related? I have to believe that the connection is something that I need to see prior to being able to solve this clue."

He finally conceded. "Yeah, okay, you're probably right. I'll start by checking to see if the symbols are by some chance on line, or more likely in one of the books that we used for the last clue. The books will mean a trip to the library, and that would have to be done tomorrow. Maybe we'll get lucky soon."

"Okay, I'm going to see if I can find anything using the location and either my ancestry or Crane's. Since I can't believe that these symbols just occurred, that would mean that someone had to create them. I want to know who and why."

"Let's plan to get together tomorrow to talk about our results. Do you think we could all meet at my mom's shop? It should be a slow day, so we can talk about things fairly easily."

"That works for me. I'll tell you what, we'll bring lunch and we can meet then. I'll text Emily and Chrissy, and we'll see you tomorrow."

We hung up and I returned my gaze out my to the stars. Were they finally starting to line up for me?

Misty jumped up onto the window seat to join me and brought me back from my dream. "Well, Mist, it looks like I've got to research to do." She curled up next to me, with her head resting on my lap as I began to search though various web sites that covered Sleepy Hollow's early history.

It was a very time consuming task to go back through the records to find out where the early settlers had claimed. By the time I had finished looking up my relatives, I was exhausted. A quick glance at the clock, and I realized why. It was almost one-thirty.

I nudged Misty, who was now sprawled out on her back sleeping, "Bed time," I said. She looked at me, yawned and closed her eyes. I tried to slide out with out disturbing her, but it didn't work. We crawled into bed and I turned out the light.

After church Sunday morning, we were sitting around the breakfast bar in the kitchen. "Guys," I said. "I found something yesterday, when I was flying with Ian and I think it has some significance to the clue. But I could really use some help here. Any chance you'd consider?"

My dad set his coffee cup down, "Stevie, we'll do anything that we can to help you with this. You know that. Now, what's up?"

"Let me grab my laptop, and I'll show you." Two minutes later, they were all looking at the overlaid symbols.

"Do you have any idea at all what the symbols are for?" Kyle asked.

I shook my head. "That's part of the problem."

"How do you know that they are connected to all of this?" Mom asked. "I mean, what makes you sure that they are part of the clue that you need to solve?"

"It comes down to, I really don't know for certain, but I have a hunch. To begin with, finding the same symbol, one in a field and the other as a result of putting three medallions together, just seems too coincidental to me. The three medallions have come to me through the clues; one for each clue. When you consider that the ratios for comparable parts are the same, the odds that they aren't related to each other get very small."

My dad was looking at the symbols on the medallions in an odd way. "What did you find, Dad?"

"Not sure. But I was thinking that some of these other symbols that are inscribed here look something like an old record." He looked up at me. "No, I don't mean those vinyl disks that we used to have music on when I was growing up.

What I was thinking was like a deed or something along those lines. It's almost like an old map."

After breakfast, my dad printed out a copy of the symbols and headed to his office to see if he could find anything that might point him into deciphering the symbols if they were in fact a deed or map. Mom headed to her office to do some computer research on the areas history.

I was getting ready to head back up to my room to take another look at where the early settlers had started out when Kyle stopped me. "Stevie, I was thinking. A witch who was upset started this whole thing. What would she want most? The answer is revenge. How would be the best way to extract it, then?"

I looked at him like a deer in the headlights. "Kyle, where are you going with this?"

"Given the approximate time period, wouldn't people always be concerned about their honor or their family's honor? What if this is the witch's way of protecting her family honor?"

"You've lost me, Kyle. What if what is her way?"

"What if the symbols are not a map, but the story? What if they tell the story of the headless horseman from her perspective?"

I was stunned. "Sheesh! Like I don't have enough to do? Now I'm supposed to try to interpret symbols into stories? We're not working with simple cave drawings, Kyle. Besides, I'm not good at that making-stuff-up-thing."

"I am," he said coolly. "Let me take a copy of that, and I'll see if I can piece it together like a story."

We walked together to my room, and I made him a print of the medallions. "I need to know which one came in which order," he said.

I showed him, and he labeled them before he left. As the door closed, I looked at the medallions sitting on my desk, and wondered what they really contained. Were they a map, a deed or a story? Maybe they were something altogether different. Regardless of how I looked at it, I had a lot to cover, and time was starting to get short.

Fumbling through the data that I had turned up about my family, I was fairly confident that the area that we had overflown yesterday wasn't where they had settled when they had arrived here. There was, however, some evidence that pointed to this being the area where Ichabod Crane's parents had settled.

Talking to Misty gave me the chance to speak my opinions out loud. "If his family settled there in the mid seventeen-hundreds, then it would make sense that he would have been intimately familiar with the area. Though, it appears that his parents would have been on the far edge of the clearing."

I studied the photographs, and compared them to the historical documents that I had been able to find. There was definitely a chance that the largest rock formation that we had seen was at the location where Crane's childhood house had stood.

"Hmm, that's an interesting coincidence then," I muttered. Gazing out the window, hoping for some inspiration, I let my mind wander a bit, again speaking aloud. "If that's where he grew up, and assuming it does actually fit with the formation at the point, then would that make the other rock formations other important features in the town? Maybe they were important pieces in the town?"

My phone rang, "Hello?" I answered.

"Hey Stevie," Emily's voice nearly sang through the receiver. "What time are we supposed to head over to meet with Ian?"

"I told him that we would be there around one. So we've got a little time. Why?"

"Thought I'd come over and we'd talk."

"Em, we're talking on the phone right now. What's the news?"

"Do you remember Wesley Bright?"

I searched my memory, "I think so. He was the tall kid that you had a crush on back when we were in, like, seventh grade. He moved somewhere in New Jersey, or something didn't he?"

"Yep! He's the one. I ran into him yesterday while I was at the mall. His folks have divorced, and so now he and his mom have moved back up this way. They're living over in Armonk now. Anyway, we saw each other at the mall, ended up having lunch together and went to see a show. He called me a little while ago, and asked if we could get together on Tuesday night. It turns out that I wasn't the only one who had a crush back then."

"Emily. What can I say other than, wow?"

Ian's mom owned and ran a small independent bookstore on the outskirts of town near the border of Sleepy Hollow and Tarrytown. As we pulled up, we could see that there were a few cars in the lot, but it was not terribly busy.

Pushing the door open, a little bell above it rang, and Ian turned and smiled at us, "Hi guys, welcome to Shelby's Shelves. There's a little table back in the corner, we can work there."

"Thanks, Ian." I led the group to the table in the back. I laid out the photos that we had taken on our flight, as well as the ones of the medallions.

"So this is what we're looking at?" Chrissy leaned over and took the two photos. "What's the big deal about them?"

I overlaid the photos. "I don't think that we could have that kind of match without there being some connection."

Ian wandered over. "Have you made any more connections about the locations of the markers?"

"Thus far, the only one that I've been able to confirm has been the original Crane house. If we assume that the other markers also indicate where things were two hundred years ago, knowing what buildings were there becomes increasingly important."

We continued to look at the photos. Every idea that we had about what else might be marked there, we jotted into a notebook. Ian excused himself several times to wait on customers, but hurried back to the group.

I'd run out of ideas much earlier, so I got up and just paced around the shop. I was hoping that some new flash of inspiration would pop into my head, or that I would suddenly see something that would tell me how to look at the pictures.

I stood at the back of the shop, staring out the front window. Emily called me, and I slowly turned and stopped mid-step.

"What is it, Stevie? Are you okay?" Emily asked, rushing to my side.

"This is going to sound ludicrous, but look at the building across the street. Do you see how most of the bricks are of a deep red color, but there are a few yellow bricks in the façade?"

When she nodded, I continued. "Look at the shape that the yellow bricks make."

"I don't see a shape."

"Play connect-the-dots with the yellow bricks." By this time, both Chrissy and Ian had joined in looking at the building.

Ian turned to me, "Holy cow! It looks like it's the same shape!"

"That's what it appeared to me as, as well. What building is that, and what is the history of it?"

Ian shrugged. "I don't know, but let's take a look at one of the books on the history of Sleepy Hollow and see if something doesn't pop out for us."

We followed Ian back to the section of local interest and he started pouring through the various books on the shelves. I kept looking out the window, at the pattern made in bricks that shared the shape of our unknown clue. There was something here that was bigger than we had ever anticipated.

CHAPTER 15:

DIGGING

Students were rushing to get to their favorite tables the following Wednesday, and I was wandering around as if in a fog. It had been four days since Ian and I had taken our flight, but other than us realizing that there was a connection between the inscriptions on the medallions, the clearing that we'd seen from the air, and the odd colored bricks that were on the building across from the bookstore, we'd made no progress.

I dropped my lunch bag on the table and pirouetted to avoid being run over by two freshmen that were racing to see who would get the better seat at the adjacent table. "I guess spring does awaken those who have been hibernating all winter." I glared over at the two who were now wrestling, pulling the chair from each other.

Sitting down, I looked around my own table. "My mom wanted me to invite everyone over for a dinner meeting tonight. My grandparents will be there and we will be trying to see if perhaps the group of us can figure out what the patterns indicate."

"What time?" Chrissy asked as she set her own lunch down.

"Dinner would be around six. You guys can come over right after school if you wanted, or whenever."

Ian looked up from the book he was poring over. "I should be able to make that. I'll have to make sure that my mom has the store covered."

"Thanks," I said. "What are you reading? It doesn't seem to be one of the fantasy books that you like so much."

He shook his head, "It's not. When my mom got back to the store on Sunday, I was still going through a few of the local interest books. When she asked, I gave her part of the explanation, saying that we noticed the pattern of the bricks, and were wondering what the history of the building was. She got me this." He held up the cover. "It's just taking a while to go through everything."

Considering the lack of progress I had made over the last few days, at least it seemed like Ian was still making strides in the finding the meaning of the symbols that we had found. Now all we needed to do was to confirm what they meant, and figure out how they fit into the overall clue.

"You got any new leads?" Emily asked taking a bite of her sandwich.

"Zilch. I've hit the wall again. Add to the lack of any progress that it is currently the last week of May, and let's just say that I'm getting real nervous."

Chrissy placed her hand on mine. "Stevie, the solstice is still three weeks away. We'll figure it out."

"You keep telling me that. But for right now, I think I'm going to have that nervous breakdown that seems to be just outside whatever door I'm at." I set down the potato chip that I was holding, and folded my hands to keep the amount that they were shaking out of everyone's attention. "I'm just getting really worried about things right now."

Emily leaned over, draped her arm around my shoulder and squeezed. "We're all going to be right there with you. You'll see. This will all be taken care of by graduation."

Graduation. The thought hit me as if I'd been punched. My parents were making all sorts of plans for graduation day, which came almost a week after the solstice. I lost my appetite.

"Stevie," Ian called. I lifted my head, but everything was blurry. "Stevie, look at me, right here." I could see a shape that I decided was most likely Ian, but I was sinking fast.

I don't have any recollection of what happened next.

"It's okay, Miss Nixon," I heard Mrs. Murphy's soothing voice.

"Where am I? What happened?"

"Well, if I had to guess, I'd say a massive panic attack. We thought my office might be more restful than the cafeteria. Just relax now, I've already called your mom and she'll be here in a few minutes to take you to the doctor's."

"But I don't want to go to the doctor's." I tried to get up, but she was able to keep me down on the cot with little trouble.

"I know you don't want to go, but it's a district policy. If someone has this kind of episode unexpectedly, they are required to be seen by a medical professional before they are allowed back into school."

"Blast it all. I just wasn't feeling well, and I feel a bit overwhelmed. I guess everything caught up with me."

"Your doctor can help you with that."

There was a knock on the door, "Mrs. Murphy?" I heard Mom's voice call.

"Ah, Mrs. Nixon. Thank you for coming. Stevie is awake and alert, and seems reluctant to see the doctor. All good signs."

Mom brushed her hand through my hair, and I opened my eyes again. "Feeling better, Honey?"

"Yeah, I guess. I'd rather not go to see the quack."

"Understandable, but required. Come on; let's get you up and out of here. We've got a group of people coming for dinner tonight." She helped me up and we headed out of the health office. I found myself wondering what I was going to tell the doctor about what had me so stressed.

Thoughts were rushing through my head that night as everyone was showing up for our work-dinner. Ian, Emily and Chrissy had all come over shortly after four, reaching the house just after Mom and I got back from the doctor's.

Chrissy was rinsing cucumbers for the salad when she inquired, "So, what's the verdict?"

"The quacks aren't exactly sure. They think it's from too much stress, so I can't even go to school tomorrow."

"Hey, where can I sign up?"

"Ian! I'd rather be there. Missing days right now isn't going to help my stress level. We've got finals coming up in a bit over a week from now. That's like the added bonus on my stress cake," I complained.

He wrapped his arms around me. "Maybe, I'll come over and play hooky tomorrow and keep you company and relaxed."

Mom gave him the evil eye. "I don't think that would be in your best interest there, Mr. Morris."

Ian chuckled. "Probably not, but I'd be willing to make the sacrifice to help out Stevie."

"Well, I appreciate your willingness, but I think I can handle being home with my daughter tomorrow just fine," she said with a wink.

The back doorbell rang, and Kyle went to answer it. A moment later, Nonni and Poppy came in. Nonni went right to work helping my mom getting everything ready. Poppy put his arm around me, "Why don't you and I take a little walk."

He led me towards my shop, "So what happened today? Your mom called and said that you had a bit of a problem at school."

"It wasn't anything to get real worried about, Poppy. I just got a bit overstressed, I think, and ended up having a panic attack at lunch."

"Stevie, my girl, I know that you're feeling like everything is coming down on you right now. But let me promise you, we will all do what we can. You need to stop worrying about things and just let them happen. If you've got to worry, worry about things that are going to make a difference."

"What am I supposed to do? Forget that there is a curse hanging over my head? Not worry about the fact that if I don't solve it within the next three weeks, I won't be around for graduation?"

He stopped and looked at me. "Is there anything else that could be done that you're not doing right now?"

"No. Not that I know of."

"Okay then. You're doing everything that you can, and so is your support group. You do need to take care of yourself. Find some time to relax a bit and get away from everything." He pointed to the shop, "Get in there and work on that plane. Get it finished. Let your mind worry about things that we can do, and the other stuff will work itself out, you'll see."

I wasn't as sure as Poppy was, but who was I to argue. Nothing more was said about my spell at school. After dinner we all headed into the family room to go over the data that we had so far.

Facing everyone, I stood in front of the fireplace, and gave them the basics. "What we've found so far, is that the inscription on the clue, the clearing that Ian and I overflew and the brick pattern on the building across from Shelby's Shelves are all the same. They have the same shape, and size ratio between points. The only conclusion that I have is that they must be related some how. The question right now is how."

"Do you have any ideas?" Nonni inquired.

"Shooting totally from the hip, I'd guess that they represent specific points. For example," I held up the photo from the flight and pointed at a specific pile of rocks. "This marker here appears to be in the same location as the original Crane house was reported to have been built on in the mid seventeen-hundreds. Unfortunately, we don't have much to go on yet for the other markers."

I motioned to the next picture, which I'd propped up on the mantle. "Further complicating things are these symbols that appear here in the picture of the medallions. These symbols aren't going to appear in nature, but I'm betting that they do have a significant role in solving this clue."

Mom got up and stood next to me, "What can we do to help, Stevie?"

I shrugged. "I think that the best thing that we can do right now is to figure out what everything means. Once we do that, we might have a chance to fully understand the clue."

Nonni's head swiveled towards me. "I thought that you'd already figured out the clue, Stevie?"

"Actually, Nonni, we figured out the puzzle. It said 'Compassion for all'. But right after we found that, we discovered this other set of symbols and how the three medallions fit together. Now we're stuck."

Emily stood up, "Mrs. Nixon and Mrs. N, why don't we work on the symbols? We can see if we can find anything in the printouts that we got from the library."

Nonni and my mom looked at each other and nodded. With Emily, they moved off to one of the tables at the edge of the room.

Poppy looked over at my dad, "Scott, why don't we take a look at the symbols as a cryptic message?"

My dad shook his head. "Actually, Dad, I think it might be a good idea for you and Kyle to take that angle. After hearing Stevie talk about the relationship to where the original house used to be, I'm thinking that maybe I should tap into some of my history books here and see if I can find any information on the architecture of that time. Maybe that would help identify the other places that are marked."

"Makes sense. What do you say, Kyle? Ready to try your code breaking skills?"

Kyle looked enthralled, "You know it."

Chrissy looked over, "May I join you?"

"The more the merrier," Poppy acknowledged, and the three of them went out to the kitchen to work at the breakfast bar.

"We're on it Stevie," Dad said as he gave me a little hug. "Do you by any chance have the coordinates of these other markers?"

"I can get them for you. They're on my GPS unit right now. I'll bring it to your…" I wasn't sure where he was going to be working.

"I'll be in my office. I've got several books on the architectural history of the area there."

"Okay then, I'll bring it there in a few minutes." Dad headed down the hall and I looked over at Ian.

He was standing by the mantle, studying the photo of the symbols intently. "What's up?"

He looked over at me. "I'm not sure. I keep having this feeling that I've seen these symbols somewhere before. I'm pretty sure I have, but I just can't figure out where."

"I have faith that you'll remember, Ian." I leaned on his shoulder and pushed myself up a bit to give him a kiss on the cheek.

"Stevie, may I borrow this for a while? I keep thinking that I saw this in a book at either my house or one of my relative's houses. It would be easier for me to match it if I had an actual copy."

I'll print one off for you while I'm upstairs getting my GPS unit for my dad."

Fifteen minutes later, I looked around. Everyone else was working on their particular point, and I was standing in the center like the supervisor. I decided to walk around between the groups.

Maybe something that I would overhear from one group would give me the information to help another group solve the puzzle.

Unfortunately, everything that I was hearing right now sounded like gibberish.

CHAPTER 16:

PROGRESS

Friday after school, we decided to head to the library to continue our work on the symbols. My dad had had little luck with locating what buildings had been where in the late eighteenth century beginnings of Sleepy Hollow, but he was still working on it. Kyle and Poppy had pretty much given up on their search for breaking the code.

So, Ian, Emily, Chrissy and I had decided that we would go back to the library and try the Special Collection room again. I was dawdling as we climbed the steps to the large main doors.

"A little slow tonight, eh, Stevie?"

I shrugged my shoulders, "I don't know, Ian. I feel sluggish and just want this to all be over."

He put his arm around my waist, "We'll figure it out. With this group, we've got a very high net IQ."

I laughed, "You're probably right."

We walked into the main room of the library, and headed to a table in the far back corner. Emily dropped her stuff on the table and headed off to find her contact for the special collections. Chrissy pulled out a seat and began piling notebooks on the table. "What are those?" I inquired.

She looked up and smiled. "I was thinking; if the symbols that we are dealing with are actually more like hieroglyphics, then it would make sense for the most popular words to appear in a certain percentage. When I went home last night, I talked to Mark for a little while. I explained that I was interested in code breaking, and he lent me some of his books from his Army days."

"Are things better between you and Mark?"

She looked up at me. "They're not great, but we're making progress. The fact that he was willing to lend me the books was a huge step."

Ian and I took seats next to each other and started looking at the preliminary data that my dad had been able to uncover. "It looks like the building across from your mom's shop was originally the mercantile."

"When did it open?"

I looked at the date that my dad had written, frowned and looked back at Ian. "It opened in 1822. Thirty years after everything else had happened."

A sound caught our attention and we turned to look towards the entrance.

"Listen, Gabby, I don't know what you think we're going to find here," Tanya was saying as she followed Gabby in.

"I've got a bunch of questions, and nobody is telling me what's what. I need answers."

The two of them disappeared into the stairwell that led to the second floor.

"Okay, that was an interesting segue," I commented and turned towards Ian. "Ian? Are you okay? You look like you're in a daze."

"What? Huh? Oh, sorry. I just remembered. I need to take care of something for my mom. I've gotta run." He grabbed his bag and headed for the door.

Emily was returning with a stack of papers that she had copied from the Special collections room. "What's going on with Ian?"

I'm sure I had a dazed look in my eye when I turned to her. "I don't know. Gabby and Tanya came in, we heard a bit of their conversation, and then he suddenly remembers that he needed to do something else."

"I wonder why he was so edgy?" Chrissy commented.

"Yeah there must be something up, don't you think, Stevie?"

I weighed my options. I knew part of what was weighing on Ian. The question was would he be upset if I told anyone else? I hoped that he wouldn't. They didn't need to know that it was actually Ian's aunt, nor that it was Gabby's mom. "Ian's been having a rough time lately. His mom's best friend has recently become quite ill. That's why he's been working the extra hours at the shop; so his mom can be there for her friend."

Focusing on the tasks at hand, we worked until nearly seven, but I felt that we had made little progress. "What is it that Ian is always saying? Something about even 'no' is an answer?" I moaned. "It doesn't seem right to use that without him being the one to say it."

Chrissy was rubbing her eyes, "Amen to that. I feel like we've been at this a whole lot longer than four hours today. I think we need to figure out what possible path there is that we've overlooked."

Emily nodded. "We must have missed something. Stevie, let's take one more look at the pictures again before we call it a night."

I spread the photos on the table, and we stared at them. I wasn't sure what it was we were theoretically looking for. "I've got to admit it, guys, I'm totally lost here. We've looked at the possibility that those symbols are hieroglyphics, a code of some kind. What have we overlooked?"

We stared at the photos for another ten minutes before Chrissy broke the silence. "I still think that they are some type of hieroglyphic. I'm just not sure for what language."

"Well, let's head off," I said and began packing my bag.

We headed out and split up. Emily was going to meet her mom at the café for dinner, and Chrissy's mom was picking her up for a family therapy appointment. I waited with Chrissy until her mom arrived.

After they left, I sat on the ledge of the library steps and let my mind wander as I texted my dad. What had I missed? What part had I overlooked?

My dad pulled up, so I put my thoughts on hold as I climbed into the car. "Thanks for picking me up, Dad."

"No problem, I was in town for a late afternoon meeting anyway. So, did you guys make any more progress on things today?" he asked as we pulled back onto the road.

"Not really. I'm wondering if we've missed something, or overlooked it at least."

"Talk it through" he said. "Maybe you'll stumble upon it on the ride."

"It's weird. I mean, our family supposedly caused harm to someone two hundred years ago. It annoys the victim's family member, who happens to be a witch. She puts some kind of wacky hex on the descendants and…" I trailed off as the new thought steeped in my mind.

"What's up, Stevie?"

"Not sure. Got an idea, though. What if the symbols on the medallions are hieroglyphs? But what if they don't translate to something in English?"

"Stevie, don't work yourself up worrying about things that most likely won't come to pass."

"No, Dad, what I'm thinking is, what if the symbols are part of her language? She was a witch, right? So what if those symbols have some meaning that would only be known to another witch?"

Dad checked the clock on the dash. "It's too late to turn around and go back to the library tonight. But the idea that perhaps this is some kind of message from something like a Wiccan spell book might have possibilities."

"I know that we don't have any resources at home, and Ian had to leave early or I'd ask him to call his aunt. But I wonder if there is anything online that might give some insight to what those symbols mean."

"There's only one way to find out," he said as we pulled into the driveway. "Happy hunting."

I jumped out of the car and dashed up to my room. I grabbed my laptop and sat down on the window seat while I waited for the computer to warm up. As soon as things finished loading, I went to Google and did a search for Wiccan symbols. It took only seconds before I found a list of sites that would show me what I was looking for.

The second site boasted an A-Z list of items that were associated with witchcraft. I clicked on it and held my breath. Moments later, the opening pages popped up and gave me a list of various items.

I pulled the photo of the three medallions out and looked at the images that we had found there. The obvious one was a big circle that went around all of the other symbols. A quick check and I found that circles represent the cycles of life and power.

I scribbled this down in my notebook. And then began to look at the other symbols. It looked like in the very center of the symbols was a smaller circle that had been quartered, with a candle set at the very center.

Searching through the list, I was able to quickly find the candle. According to the site, it meant the light and was the closest to the Divine that a human could get. The circle with a cross in it baffled me.

Trying to determine the other symbols on the three medallions was hard. Not because they were too light, but because they were more sketched lines than actual image. It looked like one might be a rocket or a broom. Another was shaped similar to a cat in mid pounce. Maybe it was a jaguar or a cougar?

The third main symbol was too hard for me to tell. It was trapezoidal in shape with a circle right on the bottom center of the largest side.

There were also two more symbols that I had no idea on. One was a like a series of three spirals that spiraled inward. The other was a long line with thin lines coming off of it. Regardless, I felt that for the first time since we had found the clue, I felt like I was making progress.

I hesitated for a moment before I pulled out my phone. Tapping the keyboard, I sent Emily, Chrissy and Ian a quick message. 'Symbols may be from Wiccan origin. Need help identifying them when we can.'

There was nothing more that I could do right now. Closing the computer, I rubbed Misty's ears until Mom called me down for dinner.

Curling back up in the window after dinner with a cup of tea, I tried to think about the unknown shapes that were on the medallions. Misty climbed back up to cuddle with me, acting like she knew that I needed that comfort to get me through. It was hard to keep my mind from reacting to today's date. There were only a few weeks left until the solstice. And once again, I was coming into the final stretch without knowing the final task.

I picked up the notebook that I had tossed on my desk earlier, and read some of my notes aloud to Misty. "We know that the clue was about compassion. But how does that relate to this task?"

Misty just looked at me and wagged her stubby tail.

I went back and started looking at the clue from the very first task. "Honest with all," I repeated. I thought to what I had to do then. "I had to be honest with everyone, especially with myself. The key to that clue was the link to me. Hmmm, I wonder."

I pulled out the second clue. "Loyalty. I needed to be loyal with my friends, and overcome any preconceived ideas that I had so that I could put my friends needs ahead of my wants."

Looking at the third clue again, "so that brings us back to this one, Misty. I need to have compassion. From the past clues, this one is going to involve me personally giving someone whom I personally have friction with the compassion that they need."

The dog's only answer was to squirm so she was closer to sitting on my lap, and leaning in so that her head and shoulder were pressing on my chest.

I scratched her ears, "Thanks, girl. I needed the hug."

She tilted her head and licked my nose. I put my arms around her and squeezed lightly. She may have only been a small dog, but she was exactly what I needed right now.

CHAPTER 17:

SURPRISES

Stepping into the school the next morning, I scanned the crowds. "Do you see Ian, Em? I texted him several times last night, but he had never responded."

"No. What's so important?"

"Guess I'm just worried, that's all. I'm hoping that his au…, um, his mom's friend is okay."

"Yeah, I can understand that. I'm sure that he is around somewhere. I'd just like to know what he was really doing yesterday while we were at the library. He's always made time for you before."

I turned and stared at her. "Emily. Look, there's nothing wrong with our relationship. It's just that Ian's had a lot going on the last few days. I'm sure that he had a perfectly good reason to run out last night."

"You're probably right, but I do wonder."

My feelings of dread were growing with every minute that passed and I didn't see him. I guess I had Emily to thank for putting those little doubts in my head.

I figured the worst-case scenario would be that I would have to wait to see him until we were in AP Physics. So, as I walked into Mr. Zuhelgger's class and he wasn't there, I nearly stopped in my tracks. Now I was sure that something was up.

"Where is Mr. Morris today, Ms. Nixon?"

I turned and saw that Mr. Zuhelgger was standing just inside the door, near where Ian and I normally sat. "I'm not really sure. I haven't talked to him since last night. He said that he had something that he had to take care of for his mom, but that was around four."

"Hmmm, well it's not like him to miss an important class, especially this close to the exam. Be sure that you take good notes so that you can help him catch up." With that, he strode to the front of the room and began his lecture.

I slumped to my seat, and tried to control the little voice that so often told me all of those doom and gloom stories that I'd hear in my head.

Carefully, I pulled out my phone, and while I looked like I was paying attention, I carefully tapped out 'Where are you? I'm worried.'

I put the phone in my pocket, and kept my hand on it so that if Ian responded, I'd be sure to get the message.

The class dragged on, and when the ending bell sounded, Ian still hadn't responded. In the hall I saw Emily talking to Chrissy. I pulled on her sleeve, "There's something very wrong here. Still no answer from him."

Chrissy turned and placed her hand on my shoulder. "I'm sure that he's fine, Stevie. Maybe his phone got damaged and he can't respond."

"Okay, that might be a possibility, but I'm still worried. Why couldn't he find someone else's phone and send a quick text to let me know."

Chrissy smiled, "Honey, it's good to see that he means that much to you. Relax. I'm positive that everything will work out in a bit."

We shuffled off towards the gym. My heart definitely wasn't up for going, and I was actively thinking about the possibility of skipping gym by going to the health office. That plan just might have worked; if I hadn't run into Mrs. Phelps.

"All set to play tennis today, Stevie?"

My stomach suddenly felt hollow. "I'm not sure that that is good idea, Mrs. Phelps. Don't you remember what happened the last time I tried tennis?"

She stopped and looked at me, "Stevie, the fact that with one stroke of your racket you put three people in the health office and injured yourself at the beginning of the year doesn't mean that you can't ever learn the game. You just need to try harder." She turned and walked away leaving me looking at the empty hallway.

"Try harder?" I asked aloud. "What does she want, for me to send the entire class to the ER?" I asked a stunned Emily. She merely answered with a shrug.

I huffed out a breathy sigh and went into the locker room.

When the class ended, Mrs. Phelps smiled at me, "Better this time, Nixon."

"Yeah, she only sent Sara to the health office after beaning her with her racket," one of my classmates said loudly.

I could feel my face flush. It had been a total accident— again. I went to swing for the ball, missed and did a pseudo-pirouette. My racket was still in my hand, spinning with me when my partner ended up a little too close and caught the racket off of the back of her head. There wasn't even any blood.

I slunk off as fast as I could, hoping that I could get out without needing to have any further conversations. For the first time that I could recall, luck was actually on my side and I made it.

French was a little better, as Emily was there to help ease some of the anxiety that I was feeling. However, the surprise quiz that Madame Lynn threw at us about did me in. "Did we ever learn how to conjugate those verbs?" I asked Emily as we were waiting for the bell to release us.

"Those were verbs? Ah, well, there goes any hope of getting a ninety in here this quarter."

"Em, I'm sure that you did fine. You always seem to figure things out when it comes to grades."

"Well, that's some comfort, I suppose." She paused and looked around at the other students who were all in some varying degrees of conversation. "Have you heard form Ian yet?"

I shook my head. "No. It's got me a little bugged and a little worried. Its'…" I paused trying to find the right words. "I don't really know how to explain it. We're supposed to be a couple, but recently it's been secrets and deception. He's ducked out on me twice now as we've been trying to figure out the last part of this clue. Even after he's promised that he's going to help. I'm worried that he doesn't feel he can trust me or something like that."

Emily rubbed my arm. "Stevie, I don't think that's it. Whenever I see him looking at you, he's got that look in his eye. I think he'd step in front of a bullet for you. He wants to protect you and get this whole curse thing behind you."

"Then why's he being so darned secretive and where is he today?"

"Let's hope that he comes in for lunch." The bell rang, and we joined the other fifteen members of our class in the exodus out the door.

Lunch was a mad house; apparently they were serving one of the school favorites for the last time this year and everybody was trying to buy lunch. "Think I'm going to go wait at the table until the line dies down a bit. Maybe I can do something productive while I'm waiting."

Emily looked at the line, "Kinda makes me wish I'd just brought a sandwich today. I hate waiting in lines."

I smiled, "Well this is probably the last time that we will ever have to wait in line for turkey and gravy day."

Panic flashed across her face. "Stevie, don't talk like that! We're going to get things worked out. We'll…Oh. Sorry. Forgot that this is the last time they're serving it this year, and this is our senior year."

"You forgot it was our senior year? Boy, you must really be under a lot of stress." I started walking into the main part of the cafeteria and angled over towards our normal table and stopped.

"What is it? Why'd you stop?" Emily asked as she nearly bumped into me.

I pointed to our table in explanation. "Ian. He's sitting at the table," I'd started walking again. "He doesn't look well, though."

Emily looked up from her phone, "Geesh, you're right. Do you think his mom's friend—"

"I don't know, but I know that right now, I need to be there for him." I walked around behind him, and draped my body over his shoulder to give him a hug.

I was surprised when he spun around and pulled me so that I ended up sitting in his lap. "I've missed you," he said as he squeezed me with a ferocity that actually scared me.

"Ian, is your aunt…" As I was asking the question, I saw Tanya and Gabby go by. "No, she's not worse. What's up?"

"I really don't want to say right now. I need you to do something for me, Stevie."

"Can you give me a hint?"

"I'll tell you everything tonight, okay? Right now, I just came into school to see you, and then I'm disappearing again for a while."

I chuckled, "You signed in late, and are going to skip this afternoon?"

"No, my mom gave me note. We have an appointment that I need to go to."

I could feel the tension building behind my eyes, I almost shouted at him, but I bit back my anger. "Ian, please tell me what's going on? I hate seeing you like this; torn up about something. I thought couples helped each other out."

He hung his head slightly, "Stevie, really there is nothing wrong with me, I promise. In fact, I think the result of the appointment will interest you greatly, as I may have a lead on those symbols."

That got my attention. "What do you mean? You're meeting with somebody about those? If so, then I should be there."

"It's not like that. I think I may have a source that can get us a book on what those symbols are. I took something that you'd said and ran a little."

"What did I say?"

"It's more what you texted. You mentioned Wicca. Witchcraft. It got me thinking, so I talked to my mom a bit—"

"Wait. You talked to your mom? About this? Ian, I really don't want this getting around, you know about me and the curse."

"Stevie, relax. I told my mom that we'd found some symbols on an old medallion that we'd come across out in the woods. She doesn't know anything about the curse. But after I explained to her what I was looking for, she said she thought that she knew where to find the answers."

"You said that you and your mom had this appointment. How are you going to explain this interest in witchcraft to whomever you are meeting?"

"I don't need to. My mom's already taken care of it." He glanced up at the line. "Come on, let's go get our lunch and then we can talk some more."

Conversation at the table bounced from topic to topic, and we never got back to what was going on about the symbols. As Ian and Emily had a quick debate on how to best solve a particular math problem, I looked across the cafeteria. I saw Tanya laughing energetically, and a rather dour looking Gabby next to her. My attention focused on them.

Pretending to eat her lunch, Gabby slouched in her chair, propping her head up with one hand. Tanya was quite animated as she talked about something with Nina, one of the other stooges that they hung around with. Neither girl seemed concerned about Gabby's mood or expression.

I watched for a few more minutes, taking side glances so that no one would see me staring. "Hey, Ian," I finally said. "Is your cousin all right?"

"What do you mean?"

Without looking in Gabby's direction, I nodded with my head in her general direction. "She's over there moving food around on her tray, but not eating. She looks like she just got a mouthful of lemon juice and is trying not to spit it everywhere. And her friends seem so oblivious to it. I was just wondering if there was something else that was up?"

He looked over, sighed, "No, not that I know of. Her mom seems to be responding to the treatments, so that's all good. I don't know. I'll ask my mom this afternoon. Maybe she has more info than I do about this, but it's probably just stress."

Seeing Gabby so depressed and Tanya being so boisterous around her, I wondered what their relationship was. I know that when I'm in one of my funks, Emily or Chrissy had always been there to help smooth the way for me. It made me wonder how Gabby's supposed best friend could act so callous around her.

I looked back to my friends, and smiled. Here at least, no matter what was going on, I had people that I could trust and count on.

"I've got to head out," Ian said as he stood. "I'll catch everyone later." He turned to me leaned down for a kiss and whispered "Check your notebook with the flower on the front. I left you something for later."

I resisted the urge to grab the binder as soon as he'd walked away. If Ian had whispered it to me, then there was a reason that he didn't want everyone else to know about this.

I watched him as he walked towards the exit. He detoured over to his cousin's table for a minute. Her expression changed from almost pain to one of annoyance. Whatever it was that was bothering her, she didn't want to share it with him.

When the bell rang, I followed the herd and made my way to Ms. Dailey's class. I dropped into my seat, and cautiously lifted the cover of my notebook.

At first, nothing popped out for me, but I started to look closer. There, taped to the inside cover, was a folded piece of paper. I pulled it off and opened it quickly.

"Dear Stevie," it read. "I know that the last few days have been crazy and I may have seemed like I was in outer space. I'd like a chance to explain everything. Please meet me tonight at 7 at 4426 Chestnut Hill Lane. I'll explain everything then. Love you, Ian."

I leaned back in my chair. What was at that address? I knew that it was really on the edge of town near Pocantico Lake, but other than that, I was lost.

Ms. Dailey walked in, and class began. But my mind was already on Chestnut Hill Lane.

CHAPTER 18:

UNUSUAL DISCOVERY

Driving my mom's car, I was struggling to find the address that Ian had given me. I finally gave up and pulled into a parking place on the side of the road. Pulling out my phone I scanned the app store, muttering to myself, "I should have brought a GPS with me."

It took about five minutes for me to find a version that would work on my phone and started back on my way.

The phone rang and I put it on speaker "Hello?"

"Stevie? It's Ian. Are you still coming?

"I'm on the way, I just took a wrong turn. I'm back on track now, so I'll be there in a few minutes."

"Okay. I just got here myself. See you when you get here."

"Talk to you in a few." I clicked off the phone, and peered out in the light rain that had begun to fall. I continued down the street, following my progress on the screen. When it said that I'd arrived at my destination, I looked around. Ian's car sat, parked in a driveway beside a hedgerow.

Confirming the address of the house, I took in the large white Victorian. Gingerbread trim that edged the windows and the porch was painted a deep maroon. The flowerbed in front of the house was beginning to bloom.

There were only a few lights on; the porch was lit as were two of the windows in the front of the house. It looked as if the rest of the house was dark and waiting for something.

A second garden sprouted on the side opposite of the driveway. I recognized some of the flowers; roses, tulips. But there were other plants that were plentiful that I had no idea what they were.

From a first impression it looked like it belonged to an elderly woman, who had taken pride in her garden.

The rain had all but stopped, so I decided to make a dash for the door. I grabbed my umbrella, and trotted towards the lit porch. I was still a few feet from the bottom step when the door of the house opened.

"Hey, Stevie," Ian greeted me.

"So, are you going to explain all of the secrecy?" I asked as I closed my umbrella.

Ian led me inside, "Sorry if it seems that I've been hiding something from you. I just didn't know that what I was looking for was in here, but I knew that I'd remembered seeing it."

"So, whose house is this?" I asked as he led me down the small hall.

Ian turned into a small alcove and descended the stairs with me following. "Technically, this house now belongs to my great uncle. I had to call him to make sure that we could get in. He's in the process of trying to decide what to do with it."

"Why? It's wonderful."

"This was my great-grandmother's house. She passed on last year, just before my dad."

"I'm sorry, Ian." I reached out and squeezed his shoulder. His hand came up to cover mine.

"It's okay. I have some really good memories of both of them here, so I find being here comfortable."

We entered into a finished basement. The ceiling was high enough that a man could stand, but lower than those in the other parts of the house I'd seen. Most of the area had been fashioned into what appeared to be a social area. A large leather couch was against one wall; a faded carpet covered the floor. Two leather armchairs, which matched the couch, sat nearly in the middle of the room, facing the couch. An entertainment center sat on the far end was cluttered with stereo components and a television.

Ian turned to me and smiled, " Great-Gran wanted the grandkids and great-grandkids to have a place to relax, so she had my uncle Bob make this little room down here for us. It allowed the adults to be upstairs having mature conversations, while the youngsters were down here wreaking havoc."

I didn't think that he'd brought me down here to show me this, "So, where are we going?"

Ian pointed to a door that was to our right. "In here." He stopped with his hand on the doorknob. "Stevie, I know that you've been through a lot over the last few months. I'm going to ask that when you go into this room, you try to keep an open mind."

"Okay. I'll try. But why?"

In answer, he pushed the door opened and hit the lights before he moved to the side.

I stood in the doorway and took in the scene. The room was moderate in size, probably ten feet square, and painted in a dark purple color. In the center of the room sat a small circular table covered with a purple cloth, but it was the crystal ball that sat proudly in the center of the table that caught my attention. "Ian?" I asked as I pointed to the table.

He shrugged. "My great-gran was a witch, Stevie. I'd known about it for years, but she never tried to push her craft on any of us. You know that one of my mom's sisters dabbles in it, but it never really clicked until the other day."

"What do you mean?"

He crossed the room to a bookshelf that sat along the wall opposite the door, and extracted a book. "Do you remember when I first saw those symbols that were on the clue? I said that they seemed familiar to me? This is why." He opened the book so that I could see. Each page was covered in drawings of various symbols, sometimes having more than ten representations for each symbol.

"Ian, what is that?"

"This is a girmoire. It's a handwritten collection of notes and practices that a practitioner of the Wiccan rite would follow. This particular book was my great-gran's and was handed down to her by her grandmother."

He stopped far a moment and ran his finger over the page in a loving manner. "If I remember the story correctly, this book is actually quite old. It seems to me that it has been passed down through generations for the last nearly three hundred years."

"Three hundred years? Really?"

He set the book on the table and crossed back to me. "When I explained what was going on to my mom, she immediately remembered about Great-Gran's girmoire. She related stories that she'd heard as a little girl that some of our relatives were actually in Salem at the time of the witch trials."

"I thought that there were no actual witches hung during that particular time."

"Oh, none were. Apparently, we did have a relative who was, but she showed no signs of having the power. Her sisters however did. They'd left Salem about a month before the trials started."

My head was spinning. "You're telling me that your relatives are witches?"

He nodded. "I'm sorry. I never really thought about it. Like I said I just made the connection the other day. When we were at the library."

I turned towards him, "You said that you needed to help your mom with something. What was going on? How did that jog your memory?"

"Stevie," he reached out and placed his hands on my shoulders. "When Gabby walked in, something in my mind clicked. I remembered a time, long ago when she and I were maybe four or five. We'd been playing down here, and Great-Gran showed us her special room. I went to my mom's shop and talked to her in private about it. Then last night, her uncle called and she was able to work out a time that we could meet him here today."

"This was your appointment?"

His eyes light up with the humor of the situation. "Yeah. This was it. I came here to meet with Uncle Bob. He let us in, and said that I could bring you here tonight."

Ian pulled out the copies of the photos that I'd made for him the other night and set them on the table next to the book. "Shall we?" he asked.

I nodded and pulled out one of the old wooden chairs that sat at the table. We began by looking at the symbols that we could see on the medallion. "This one could be either a tree or a broom," I said pointing at one of the symbols.

Ian scanned the symbols shown in the book. "It looks a lot like this one here, don't you think?" he asked showing me a picture from the book.

Sure enough, the image that had been inscribed in the metal looked surprisingly like the inked version in the book. "Looks like it to me. Let's see, that would make it a broom, right?"

"Yep. And according to the scrawl here, it says that a broom is used to represent the ability to rise above the earthly plain. Sheesh, that's not exactly going to be a huge help with this."

"Thanks for the confidence, Ian. That was the medallion that I found in the woods near the mall. So, that would be the one from the second task. Loyalty."

"Okay. So far, nothing is jumping out at me, but let's keep going. This one here," he said pointing to the latest medallion "looks like an animal."

"That's what I thought. But it doesn't look like the hound that we saw on the second clue."

"Then let's see if it's a cat."

"That makes sense, I suppose. If we're talking about a witch, it would only seem natural for her to have a cat."

"Here it is. And the note here says that the cat represents the ability to perceive beyond the physical world."

"Now I'm stumped. I have no idea how that goes into the rest of the clue, or what the next image is."

We studied the odd shaped image, turning it in all directions. "Maybe this one isn't in the book?" I suggested.

"Maybe we need to go through the book and see if we can find a match."

Thirty minutes later, Ian leaned over and pointed, "What about this one here? It looks pretty close."

I looked at the photo and the drawing he pointed to. "Could be. What is it supposed to be?"

"A bell, which represents the great Goddess who purifies."

"Wonderful. Now what exactly does that mean?"

Ian looked at the handwritten text. "Doesn't give much more than that here, but if nothing else, we have a starting point for further investigation. What else do we have?"

"Well, from the medallion that I got at the end of the first task, there's a duck in the center of the spiral."

"I'm not seeing a duck here, but that might mean that it is a symbol from something other than Wiccan. What is the symbol in the other one?"

"It's kind of hard to explain. It looks like one of the crosses that my mom makes out of palm leaves every Easter."

"I'm not seeing that one here either," Ian grimaced.

"Here's a thought. We know that the hound was the Celtic symbol for loyalty. Maybe these other two are Celtic in origin as well.

"That's a distinct possibility. We can hit the library for that tomorrow."

We continued to look at the girmoire for another forty minutes. By the time we had finished, we had located a candle in the center which we guessed meant divinity, and a circle with a cross in the center, which was the Wiccan symbol for Earth.

When he closed the book, Ian looked over and smiled at me. "Well, Stevie, it looks like we've made a bit of progress tonight."

I looked at the folded paper that I now held in my hand, covered with notes from our session. "We've been able to identify most of the symbols on the medallions. It's hard to believe how many they put into one small picture."

"If I counted right, there were twelve symbols that are there."

"Twelve? That can't be right, can it?"

"Well, we have the obvious ones that we identified earlier: duck, hound, cross, cat, broom, bell, candle, and Earth. But did you notice what the overall shape was? It's a pentagram. And see just inside, there is a faint circle."

"That's only…" I paused to count, "ten. What else am I missing?"

"It's only a guess, but I think that the spirals around each clue also play into this. I seem to remember Great-Gran talking about them as a kind of journey. And did you notice that the three clues came together in some kind of shape?"

"Yeah, but I just figured that, you know, three clues, three legs."

"That may be it!" Ian pulled out his phone and went to a search page on the Internet. "Bingo! The three legs is one way to show a triskelion."

"A who?"

"It's called a triskelion. From what they show here, it can have several forms, including something that looks very close to what we have."

"So what does it mean?"

He thumbed through a few points and looked up. "Honor. It's a symbol that is both in Celtic and Wiccan culture that means one's honor."

"Ian, this may be a bad time to mention this, but have you noticed that all of the clues have been about one word: honesty, loyalty, compassion. If this symbol means honor, than does that mean that there is really a fourth task?"

He thought for a moment. "It may. I think we need to plan to come back and do a bit more research here. I have a feeling that there may be some more hidden in this."

"Did your Great-Gran happen to have a book on numerology?"

"Not sure, but we can start there on the next time."

We headed up the stairs. At the top, Ian led me through a small sitting room to the kitchen where he had assembled a few snack items. As we nibbled on the cookies I looked around at the various wall hangings that were displayed. My eyes fell on one in particular.

"Is this your family tree, Ian?"

"The part from my mom's side, yeah." He reached over my shoulder and touched a name. "Samantha here is my Great-Grandmother; this is her house. Why?"

"This name here, McCrayn? This is the surname of Icabod Crane's great-grandfather. This would likely be the name of the witch who cast the spell."

"Wait. You're saying that I'm a direct relative of the witch who caused all of this?"

CHAPTER 19:

NEXT STEPS

Stunned to the point of not being able to talk, Ian staggered back until he collapsed in a heap on one of the wooden chairs. "Stevie, this can't be. I can't be related to the person who has messed up your life this past year."

I walked over to him. "Ian, you're not responsible for what happened in the past." I knelt down on the floor in front of him, took his hand and looked into his eyes. "Look, maybe this is how is was always supposed to end. I can't say that I'm thrilled about what happened two hundred years ago between our relatives. But here we are today, working together to finish this."

"If anything happens to you, I'm never going to be able to forgive myself."

This concerned me more than anything else that he had said. "Ian, we will find a way to work this out. I'm depending on you to help me through this."

He squeezed my hands and closed his eyes, sobbing softly.

Talking to keep Ian calm, I rummaged through the cabinets and located some tea bags. They didn't go bad did they? I hoped not, as I filled the teakettle and set it on the stove.

Going back over to Ian, I sat on his lap, and hugged him as tight as I could. "Ian, listen to me. You are the most generous, loving guy I've ever met. You didn't have anything to do with the events that happened."

"I know," he sniffled. "It's just that I can't believe that my however-many-greats aunt would do something like this. If she was Wiccan, or whatever it was called then, what happened to the whole thing about not harming anyone? This curse? It stands to cause harm, and if what we found at the beginning of all this is correct, it has harmed others. It's killed them, Stevie. How am I supposed to live with that knowledge?"

"The same way I'm going to. We're going to utilize the information that we have available to us now, and figure out how to totally solve this last clue. Then, I'm going to complete the task and break this curse once and for all."

The tea kettle sang and I fixed our tea and brought the cups back to the table.

He looked up at me, and our eyes met. For the first time since he'd learned about his heritage, he smiled. "You're right. We're going to find the way to make this happen." He looked over at the wall hanging, and made a fist. "When you were given this curse, you were told that you had to prove yourself to be stronger than your ancestor. You were going to have to face choices and make decisions that would help right the wrongs that he did so many years ago. I now have the same challenge. What she did, she did out of anger, and now I must help you find a way to break this curse. To right the wrong that she did against your family."

What could I say? So I did the best thing that I could think of. I kissed him. When his arms came around me, I sighed aloud, nearly purring like a happy cat.

Sitting back down, I pulled out the notes that I had made while we had been in the basement. "Shall we begin by trying to figure out what else the clue may be trying to lead us to?"

"I think my brain has had enough abuse for one night. I'm not sure I'd be very helpful right now. Why don't we let it sit until tomorrow, and then we can take another stab at this?"

"You're probably right," I admitted. "I don't think it's going to hurt too much to let it sit for right now." I didn't realize it, but unconsciously I began to wring my hands.

"Stevie, I know that the solstice is only days away right now. We'll figure this out." When I looked over at him, he just sighed. "I'm sorry, it's just this whole thing just sucker punched me. I think I need a day to let it sink in and help me get my thoughts in order. I am going to do everything that I can to help you with this, believe me."

"I know, Ian. It's just that the closer we get to the solstice, the more anxious I become."

"I can understand that," he replied. After a pause he continued, "I've gotten nervous with the last two deadlines. Something tells me that this one is going to be even worse. Just realizing the connections—"

"Connections," I whispered. "I think you might be onto something there."

"What? What are you talking about?"

"I'm beginning to think that all of this is about the connections. My ancestors and yours, you and me, it's all about the connections and the choices that we each make."

Chimes from the clock in the hall rang out. "Is it really nine-thirty already?" I asked surprised.

"I didn't realize that it had gotten that late. I'd hoped that after we looked at the book, that perhaps we'd go somewhere for a little ice cream. I guess we'd better get ready to head out."

I took our cups to the sink and washed them. I placed the tea bags into a plastic baggy that I placed in my purse. When I saw Ian's curious glance, I smiled. "Since no body lives here. It makes more sense to take things with us and throw them out somewhere else."

"See, you're still thinking. I'm about useless right now."

"That's not true. Why don't we hit Scoop's on the way home and we can enjoy that ice cream and maybe I can bounce some ideas off of you?

"That will only work if the ideas are wrapped in a rubber ball. Even then, I'm not sure how much bounce I can give, but we can try.

Driving my car back to Scoops, I took advantage of the hands free set up and made a quick call. "Hi, Mom?"

"Stevie! What's up honey? I expected you to be home about a half hour ago."

"We got caught up with a few things. Listen, Mom, I'm wondering if you can help me with a few things?"

"What do you need?"

"Well, it turns out that the address that Ian gave me was his Great-Grandmother's house. She was apparently, well, she was a witch."

"Really? She thought she was a witch?"

"I'm not really how she saw herself, or if she had powers or not. But we found something quite interesting. It turns out that Ian's descended form the McCrayn family."

"Wait. Stevie, are you saying that Ian's great-grandmother is a descendent of the legend as well?"

"It sure seems so. When we saw that, he was taken totally by surprise. He had no idea."

"I can see that. Now, you said you wanted me to do something for you. What did you need?"

"Mom, I was wondering if you could do a little research for me on numerology?"

"Numerology? What's that for?"

"One of the things that we found tonight. I have this sinking feeling that this curse isn't going to end with the completion of the third task."

"But, everything that you've shown us says that there were just three tasks."

"I know. But with one of the symbols that we identified, I've got this feeling that there is more than just three now.

Please, can you look up information on Wiccan practices and special numbers?"

"Sure, Honey. We can go over it when you get home, okay?"

"Thanks, Mom. I'm stopping off at Scoop's with Ian for a quick ice cream, hoping that I can give him the support that he needs to steady himself, and then I'll be home."

Mom was waiting for me in the family room when I got in. "How did things go with Ian, Honey?" she asked.

"I think he's doing better. It's all getting so complicated."

My dad came in with his cup of coffee and a coke. Handing me the coke, he sat next to my mom on the couch, "So what did you find that has your Mom looking at numerology?"

I sat in the rocking chair and pulled my knees up to my chin. It took nearly fifteen minutes for me to give them the basic run down on what had happened. "So, when Ian recognized the triskelion and said that it was a symbol for one's honor I got to thinking; every clue thus far has had a single word. Honesty, loyalty, compassion and now, honor; I think that there is a fourth task involved."

Mom looked at Dad and then to me, "It seems that you may be on to something there, Stevie. When I looked up the numbers, I found that the number three is considered to be a sacred number. However, some sites note that the number four is the number of completion."

"The number of completion?" I repeated. "That would make sense. Three main tasks that are main pillars of society, but in reality, it's the fourth that completes the entire picture."

"Any ideas on what you're going to have to do?" Dad asked.

I shook my head, "Not yet." Somewhere in the depths of my brain things were beginning to form, but they weren't clear enough yet for me to hazard a guess at. "I think that we are on the right track. The idea that there was a fourth was a shock to me, and to be honest, I never would have found it…"

"What are you thinking about?" Mom asked as I trailed off.

"I was thinking about Poppy's Bible. When we went through it back in September, there was someone who had made it through to this last step. I think they missed the last clue, the fourth clue."

"What were you going to say a minute ago, before your thoughts went here?" Dad asked.

"I was thinking, that I never would have made this connection, to the fourth clue, if it hadn't been for Ian. It was his connection that allowed me to make it."

"Well then, I think we need to be thankful that fate put him into your path."

I looked at Dad. "That's a little unusual for a dad to say about his teenage daughter's boyfriend, isn't it?"

He winked at me. "Maybe, but I'd rather think that because of this connection, you'll be the one to break this curse."

I went over to the couch and did something that I hadn't done since I was a little girl: I snuggled in between my parents.

Leaning against the window jamb later, I called Emily. I hadn't talked to her since right after school today, and I was sure that she was curious as to how things had gone. I filled her in about what had been found, and then we started to brainstorm ideas about what some possible answers might be.

"It might be as simple as now that you've figured out that there is a fourth clue, it's done," Emily said.

I gave Misty's ear a rub, "I don't think so, Em. I really don't think that it will be that easy. The best that I can figure it so far is, the first three tasks were focused on the building of criteria that every civilized culture in the world puts heavy consideration on."

"What do you mean?"

"Well, it's just, everyone wants to be known as an honest person. Every culture rewards the loyalty of its people. We've been taught from a very young age to be compassionate, I mean, the whole do unto others bit, right?   But when it's all put together, what do you have?"

"But how does the honor card fit in?"

"I'm not really sure. I mean, in many cultures isn't it death before dishonor? If we use that as a base, wouldn't that indicate that honor has to be held in high esteem?"

"Maybe. Listen, why don't we get some sleep, and we can figure this out tomorrow. Maybe we'll get some ideas while we catch some zees."

"Okay. Catch you in the morning." I hung up and gazed out at the stars. My time on this task was running out very quickly. I needed to have some insight to this, and I really could use it now.

I heard a soft snore, and looked down at Misty who was now asleep, her head propped on my foot. "Come on, girl. Let's get some sleep."

Sleep came easily that night, and with it came the extremely vivid dreams that I had been having since the beginning of all this. I was back in the clearing, but it wasn't the same witch that I had seen in times past. This one was younger, with blond hair. Her cheeks were stained with tears.

"A smart lass, you are. Your thoughts and questions have brought you far. Now this curse is left for you to break, but more than just your life is now at stake. For those whose souls on this plane are trapped, we pray thee follow the clues given you on the map. Do your duty; make your family proud, for honor is more than just a colored shroud. Do not wrap yourself in lies, for it is in your heart where the answers thrive. Go now my friend, believe in yourself and know that in you, you will find the end."

She looked at me with eyes that were the same color as Ian's: ice blue. But her eyes begged me to find the answer. "Please, can you show me the way? What do I need to do to solve the fourth task? Is it the last one?"

She shook her head, "I cannot answer the questions you ask, but you know all of the tasks. We have given you the way; you've seen the map. Take your time, follow your heart, but beware of traps. Success is in you, this we've seen. You have the power to destroy this hell where we've been. As I leave, a gift I give. A cure for doubt, one to help you live. When confused say this thrice; 'My honor is who I am for the rest of my life'. The way will be clear. Rest now; gain strength for the end is near. Remember, 'My honor is who I am for the rest of my life, my honor is who I am for the rest of my life, my honor is who I am for'…" Her voice faded with her image.

I found myself standing in the clearing alone, yet not alone.

Walking to the large rock that had been placed as a tribute to Crane, I laid my hand on it. It was warm to the touch, despite the night air. I found myself wondering if this was to be the final location for the last task. "I am the one who will break this curse.

You believed in harm to none, but in your anger you've cursed more than mine. All of us suffer; so it is through me, with your kin to help, that we will finally put you all to rest. My word I give you here on this sacred ground."

A glimmer caught my eye, a purple crystal lying on the ground. Picking it up, I studied it and placed it on the center of the boulder. My own homage to what was to come.

CHAPTER 20:

FINALS

Feeling slightly nauseous, I opened my eyes. The dream about being in the clearing again was much too vivid. I pulled the blankets in around me closer, and even the thought of getting out of bed made me feel uncomfortable. I wondered if it had only been a dream, or if I had actually gone to the clearing last night.

From the security of my cocoon of blankets, I wriggled my hands free enough to grab the pen and note pad from my nightstand. I closed my eyes and willed the scene from the dream to come back as clear as possible. I noted every detail that I could.

I wrote out the soliloquy that the witch had given me. I tried to put everything down word-for-word, or at least as close as I could with what had happened.

When I finished, I re-read everything, committing it to memory and at the same time testing it, seeing if there was anything that I'd forgotten.

Misty stretched and yawned, her little stub of a tail wagging as she plodded across the bed to come say her good mornings.

"That was one weird dream, Misty," I said as I stared out the window.

Mom knocked on my door, "I heard you talking to Misty. Is everything all right?"

"I think the closer we get to the solstice, the weirder the dreams are getting."

"Why don't you tell me about it?" she asked, sitting on the edge of my bed.

When I finished relaying the story, she rubbed her hand across my face, smiled and said, "I think you've got some of the answers in there. It's time to find them." She rose and headed down to start breakfast.

Confused, I made my way to the window and sat on the bench. I pulled my knees up and rested my chin on them. "What did she mean that I've got the answers?" I pondered aloud.

I re-read the page from the notebook. If I understood her correctly, somewhere on this page laid the answer that I was looking for. I went through it line by line, but nothing seemed to pop out.

I needed to get ready for school, so I set the note down, and headed for the bathroom. All through my shower and the time I spent getting dressed, I continued to run the conversation through my head. There were at least a few possible glimmers by the time I made it downstairs.

Kyle and my dad were sitting at the breakfast bar. Kyle was plowing his way through a pop-tart and a bowl of cereal while Dad had opted for oatmeal and a bagel. I pulled up a chair, and plopped into it, and Dad looked up from his paper. "Rough night, huh?"

"And then some," I told them.

"What happened?" Kyle asked through a mouthful of pop-tart.

As Mom placed a bowl in front of me, I gave them the rundown of the dream. "I think that there may be a few areas where I've made some progress, but I don't know.

Dad sipped his coffee, "Tell me some of your thoughts."

"Well," I pondered for a moment, "I'm beginning to think that if I don't make this deadline, that it will be more than me who pays the price."

"I'll miss you, Stevie. Can I have the bigger bedroom?" Dad flipped his paper at Kyle, and we all laughed.

"What I mean is when the dreams first began, it was an elderly witch who was set against me trying to survive. Recently, there have been others; ones who are trying to help me. I think that they are prisoners of this curse as well. They can't show me the way, but she kept saying that they, plural, had given me a map."

"What map?" Mom asked as she brought over her tea to join the conversation.

"That's it. I don't have a map."

Kyle paused, and stared into his cereal bowl. "Poppy, Chrissy and I looked for a map. Some of the locations appeared to have some connection to the legend, but not all of them. Maybe it's a list of what has to be done in a specific order."

We all stared at him. "What?" he demanded.

"Kyle, I think you may be onto something there." I jumped up and rushed to my purse to retrieve the photo that I had there. "It's closer than running up to my room. If we follow Kyle's idea, then the individual symbols tell me where to go and what to do."

We talked through various ideas until it was time for us to head for the bus.

Mom walked over to me as I was stuffing a few things into my purse for the day.

"Not taking your book bag?" she asked.

"School's over now, Mom. Today is the last day of classes before exams begin. A week from Friday is graduation."

"I know, Honey. Just like I know that Prom is this Saturday, and the solstice is Sunday."

My heart nearly stopped. I was down to four days, counting today, until my deadline hit. I swallowed hard, "I'm confident that we're going to get this done, Mom. We'll take some special pictures of all of us at Graduation."

I gave her a quick hug and rushed out the door. Emily was standing at the walk, dressed more like she was heading to the pool rather than school.

"Figured I'd be comfortable today, seeing as it's the last day before…Stevie, what's wrong?"

"It's Sunday, Emily." I blurted out.

"No. Pretty sure that today is Wednesday. Last day of school, Field Day's this afternoon."

"No, no, no," I whined. "I mean the solstice. It's this Sunday. I just realized how close it was, and how far I still need to go."

Emily put her arms around me. "We haven't missed yet, Stevie, and I don't see any reason to start now. From what you said last night, you and Ian made some significant progress last night. It's just a matter of putting the time in, and then it'll be like," she snapped her fingers, "a snap to finish."

I forced myself to take several slow, cleansing breaths. I started to relax bit by bit. "Thanks. I guess the date kind of surprised me, and I just went into full panic mode."

"Well, we'll have to dock your pay for it then," she quipped.

I smiled, relieved that the worst of the anxiety had left. For now at least.

Emily smiled at me, "Better?"

"I think so. Thanks, Em." We started off to the bus stop. "I had another one of those dreams last night."

Emily looked concerned. "Everything all right?"

"Who knows really? I feel okay, I guess. Just real confused."

"Did she, you know the witch, did she try to hurt you?"

"No. What really surprised me was that it wasn't the same witch who had been doing all of that before. This one was younger; sadder almost. She talked about helping me."

"Well, if she was going to help you, why didn't she tell you how to break the bloody curse?"

"Maybe she did."

Emily's head snapped towards me. "What do you mean?" she asked as we reached the edge of the crowd at the bus stop.

I looked around hoping that we would see Chrissy here, but after her coming out in March, her mom had decided it was safer for her to drive Chrissy to school. "I'm not really sure how to best describe it. I wrote up what I could remember of the conversation that we had——"

"You talked to her? Did she give you instructions then?"

"She said that she couldn't tell me the answers, but that, and I quote, 'they had given me the map' and that should help."

"What map? I don't remember you having any such map?"

"When I told my family about it over breakfast, Kyle thought that maybe it's the symbols on the medallions."

The bus lumbered up the hill and stopped. "I guess that that is something to work with." As we waited in queue, she turned to me with a grin, "Maybe we should ditch classes this morning."

Skipping classes that morning didn't sound like a very good way to start our very last day of being students in Sleepy Hollow High. I actually felt a pang of grief as I walked to my locker. "What's up, Stevie?" Ian asked, as he leaned on the locker next to mine.

"Just thinking; this is the last morning I'll come to this locker. After today, we aren't allowed to use the lockers, and next year some freshman will move into it for their four years here."

"I can buy that as part of the reason you look so dazed, but I think that there may be more."

"Fine," I agreed in an exasperated tone. "It's been a long morning already. I realized that the solstice is this Sunday, and that was after I had last night's sleep interrupted by another one of those vivid dreams."

Concern flooded his face. "Are you okay? Did she, my great-aunt or whatever she is, hurt you?"

I reached up and placed my palm on his cheek. "I'm fine, Ian. Besides, it wasn't the old witch that has been causing most of these dreams. This one was younger, and claimed that she was trying to help."

"Really? That's a relief that maybe my family tree didn't rot due to Hester and her screwed up ideas."

"Hester?"

He sighed. "After our little discovery last night, I talked to my mom. We went through several books that had the family history. Best guess is that the witch that would have been the one that put the curse on you was Hester McCrayn."

"It's nice to know who's been causing me grief for the past year. But, I'm going to hope that whomever it was last night was right. She claimed that they have given me a map to help me solve this and break the curse."

The warning bell rang, Ian looked at me. I could see the questions in his eyes, but there wasn't time right now. "We'll all talk about it at lunch. I think we're closer than we ever thought."

The day flew by, and it seemed that before I was ready, I was saying good-bye to my teachers. I walked through the halls, now deserted by the students who had all rushed out to the field behind the school for a picnic lunch to be followed by our traditional Field Day events.

Ian stood with Chrissy and Emily near a small picnic table that was shaded by a large maple tree. "Hey, Stevie," he said as he gave me a quick kiss. "Well, it's official, we don't have any more class."

"Ha. Cute joke," I said as I pulled up a seat. As we dug into our hamburgers and chips, I retold the story of my dream, again, and finished up with Kyle's thought about the map. "So, I'm open to any ideas that might get us there."

Ian was thoughtful, while Emily sat with her eyes closed. Chrissy popped a chip in her mouth, "I think Kyle is probably right. Whenever we found one of the medallions, it was associated with you having a vision of a witch, but not the one who's been plaguing you in these dreams."

I watched Ian cringe. He hadn't yet told them of the connection between him and Hester yet. "I wouldn't say that I've been plagued. But you're correct. With each of the medallions it has been a different witch."

"Do you have the photo of the medallions, Stevie?" Emily inquired.

"Yeah," I said pulling it out of my purse. "Here it is."

"Okay, let's go through the symbols mean one more time," Ian said.

We went through them one at a time, listing them down in the notebook. "We were right about the other symbols being Celtic, and what we thought that they stood for," I said.

Ideas were batted around by everyone, but I sat quiet. The witch from my dream had said that I had the answer "For it's in my heart where the answers thrive," I said softly.

Conversation around the table stopped. "What was that?" Emily asked.

"I was thinking about what she said. It's in my heart where the answers thrive. I think this might be the key."

Chrissy was getting flustered, "That stupid old witch who did this should just rot," she snapped.

I snuggled in closer to Ian, and held his hand. "Let's not make the same mistake here. Let's work the problem. I think that if we…" I trailed off.

"Stevie?" Ian was suddenly concerned. "Stevie, what's going on?"

"I think I've got it. She was right, it is right here."

"Want to share with the rest of the class?" Emily prompted.

"The three tasks: Honesty, loyalty and compassion. The duck, the hound and I'm pretty sure the cross on the medallions is actually a Brigid's cross. They are all part of what makes us who we are. We are judged by how honest we are, how we treat our friends and our compassion to others. But where does it all come from? From inside us. If we help someone, with out looking for repayment, people say that we have a good heart. The answers come from in my heart. That's what she said."

"Okay," Ian said, sounding slightly dazed. "Keep going."

"Well, let's see, by looking at the spirit of someone, as opposed to their earthly body, we see them for who they are," I nodded towards Chrissy. "That's what we decided that the broom was for. The cat which is the ability to perceive beyond the physical world would indicate that one is required to look beyond what we see right now. It's similar to compassion."

I paused to take a drink. My hands were shaking now, not from nerves, but from excitement. "The bell stands for the goddess who purifies. Wouldn't that be along the lines of forgiving someone or something that has caused us pain? The candle represents the divine, what we are all trying to obtain in life. All of these combine to help shape the way the world evolves."

Ian looked over, "The circle with the cross. All that's left is the triskelion."

"And that one is easy. When you do what's in your heart; be honest, loyal and show compassion. When you forgive others, look beyond yourself, and strive for divinity what you have is a strong sense of honor. You understand right and wrong, and do what ever it takes to make the world right."

There was silence when I finished. I was suddenly concerned and then it seemed to hit everyone. "Stevie, I think you've nailed it," Emily said.

Chrissy nodded, "I can't see any flaws in that logic. Ian?"

"I'd agree with that. Now all we have to do is help you find a way to accomplish it all."

"Theoretically, that should be easy. I just need to be who I've always been. I'll just need you guys to help keep me steady, because my intuition that just kicked in tells me that there is a disaster waiting right around the corner."

CHAPTER 21:

PROM

Looking at myself in the mirror, I was having trouble believing that it was me staring back. The girl, no, young woman, that was there was gorgeous. Her hair was done up in an elegant twist, that left tendrils framing her face. Her gown of soft pink was exactly the right tone to bring her normally pale face to life and looking vibrant.

Emily rushed in, "Stevie, you've got to see this," as she pulled me towards the window.

Looking out, I saw the sleek gray limo that was now parked in front of my house. The driver in his black uniform made his way to the rear doors and held them open for the three passengers to exit.

Wesley Bright, who was now officially dating Emily, climbed out of the car. "Em, he looks so cute in the black tails. Does he have a top hat to go with them?"

She poked me in the ribs and laughed. "Actually, yeah, he does."

Chrissy walked into the room. She was dressed in a light blue dress. "Are the guys here yet?"

"They just arrived."

"Wonderful!" she nearly danced over to the window to look out.

I had to admit, I'd been a little nervous when I found out that Chrissy had a date for tonight. Nothing against her, but I wasn't sure how a transgendered girl found a date for her senior prom. It turned out that one of the other members of her support group was her escort tonight. According to Chrissy, Trevor was a thoughtful bi-sexual guy, who had no problem with her being trans.

"Oh there he is!" Chrissy squealed.

"He looks so proper wearing the traditional black tux," Emily said. Turning to Chrissy she continued, "You guys are going to have a great night. I'm so happy for both of you."

They continued their conversation, but my attention was riveted on the figure dressed in a dove gray tux with the light pink vest.

One look at Ian, and my mouth actually watered. He looked good enough to eat.

"Looks like somebody else is really excited about tonight," Emily said to Chrissy as she nudged me.

"I can't help it. I've been thinking about this for years, and now it's here. Our senior year is almost over, and we're about to have the best summer…" my voice trailed off. We all looked at each other not saying the words, but each understanding.

Chrissy reached out and placed her hand on my shoulder, "It's going to be all right, Stevie. Enjoy tonight, make it the memory that you can carry for the rest of your life."

"If I don't figure things out, it will be among the last things I do."

"Stevie! You've come this far with that stupid curse thing, you've got to believe that you'll figure it out."

I walked over to my dresser, and fingered the three medallions. No matter how hard I tried, there was going to be one fact that I couldn't forget. The summer solstice was tomorrow. The question was would I see it?

"Considering how much we've looked forward to tonight, and that I've done everything that I can, I'm making this vow: I'm going to thoroughly enjoy every aspect of tonight."

As Chrissy and Emily came over and joined in a group hug, I could hear the voices from downstairs carry up.

The knock on my door preceded my mom's entrance by a second. "Girls! You all look so lovely! Are you ready? I can tell you that the three young men downstairs are."

"I think we are, Mrs. Nixon," Emily said as she dabbed her eye with a tissue.

"Stevie," Mom said as she came over and pulled me close. "You look absolutely stunning tonight. I want you to put everything, but the enjoyment of the prom, out of your head. Remember who you are, and keep true to that. You've always made us proud of you. Keep your head up, and be strong." She kissed me lightly on the cheek, and led me out of the room.

Leaning into Ian's strong shoulder as we swayed on the dance floor, I let my fingers play in the ends of his braid. I nuzzled my head into the space between his neck and shoulder, and the feel of his hands sliding up and down the back of my dress caused me to nearly purr.

"What are you thinking about, Stevie?" he asked softly.

"Just trying to memorize everything. Dinner was exquisite, now dancing with you."

Giving me a squeeze, Ian said, "This has been one of the most memorable days of my life. I wish my dad could have been here to see me all spiffed up, but even that can't take the shine off of tonight."

We spun around for a few more songs, and then went back to our table. I joined Chrissy and Emily while Ian went for some soft drinks.

"Is this everything that you hoped for?" I asked my friends.

"More than," Chrissy said with a wry smile. "I never thought I'd make it to prom, now look at me in my awesome dress with a cute guy for a date. It's almost perfect."

"It sure is," Emily added. "How are things going for you?"

"It's been wonderful," I gushed.

A commotion from a few tables away caught my attention, along with everybody else's. Tanya had just jumped up, hands covering her mouth and her eyes wide with excitement. Her eyes darted over to where Gabby sat, alone at a table near ours.

"I wonder what she's up to?" I muttered.

"With that look? Nothing good. That's the look she has when she finds out some really juicy gossip on somebody. Gossip that is going to cause somebody serious problems," Emily stated.

Without preamble, Tanya and a few of her cronies marched over to the table where Gabby sat. "Her best friend?" Chrissy said softly. "I expected her to go after someone, but usually those two are peas in a pod."

"Usually," I agreed. Memories flashed back of several times over the last few months when they weren't together. "Maybe something's been brewing with them. They haven't been hanging together as much."

Their voices were quieter than I expected, but if I allowed myself to be rude, I could hear most of what they were saying.

"Who are you?" Tanya demanded.

"What are you talking about?" Gabby pleaded.

"You know darn well. You never told me about your dad having problems at work. You barely admitted that your mom was sick, and now to find out that you're knocked up? I guess I spent the last few years hanging out with a stupid slut!"

"What are you talking about? I'm not the one who's been sleeping with half of the football team!"

"Maybe not, but you're the one who's in trouble."

At my own table, the three of us looked at each other. "Oh, boy," I whispered, getting nods from the other two.

Ian, Wes and Trevor came back carrying drinks. "What's going on there?" Trevor asked.

"Ian," I said, "You may want to try to help your cousin. I think she's in a sticky spot."

"That may be hard, considering she just ran to the ladies room." He pulled up a chair, and leaned in, "Care to tell me what I missed?"

I gave him the short version of what I'd overheard. He simply shook his head, "Uncle David has been questioned about the missing funds. It isn't making life any easier for her, or for Aunt Annie. Of course, Gabby is on probation, so if she is pregnant, that is going to make life so much more stressful for her and her folks."

"Seems like they have a pretty full plate right now," I said gripping his hand. "Does she have anyone she can lean on right now?"

"I would have thought Tanya, but it appears that she's the one leading the offensive against Gabby. So, I don't think so."

Watching Tanya follow Gabby towards the ladies room, with a group of girls behind her, my heart sank. "I think there's going to be trouble. Maybe we should get someone?"

Ian turned and looked in the direction that I was pointing. "Blast it all! I'm going to go get Mrs. Lerch and get her caught up and headed this way." I watched as he nearly jogged off.

"Em, Chrissy? I think it's time for a ladies room run," I said standing.

"Um, Stevie, I can't," Chrissy said sheepishly.

I'd forgotten that the school, while allowing Chrissy to be herself, had insisted that she only use specific bathrooms. When Mrs. Lerch and learned that Chrissy was coming to prom, arrangements were made for her to use a specific bathroom here as well.

"Sorry, Chrissy. Em?"

"You want to voluntarily go in there? Into the same small room where at this very moment, Tanya and Gabby are?" She rose slowly and motioned with her hand, "Insanity, here we come."

A crowd of girls stood around the small alcove, while two voices echoed off of the tiled walls.

"Can't keep hiding, you slut!" Tanya shouted.

I stood on my tiptoes and could barely make her out. She was surrounded by the normal contingent of girls, all of whom were watching the showdown eagerly. Gabby was sitting on the floor cowering, tears streamed down her face.

"What's going on in here?" Mrs. Lerch demanded as she swept into the bathroom.

The mob of girls that had been standing on the perimeter, suddenly felt that they'd seen enough and made a mass exodus, leaving Gabby, Tanya and her entourage, Mrs. Lerch, Emily and me.

"Miss Spitz? Would you care to tell me what's going on?"

Tanya's glare never left Gabby, who was still huddled on the floor.

"It seems, that my ex-best friend has been making the moves with my boyfriend, and spreading some viscous rumors about me behind my back."

"That's not true!" Gabby protested. "I never even—"

"You'll have your turn, Miss Sosong." She turned to look at the two of them; Gabby huddled on the floor with her makeup streaked from tears and Tanya standing with her fists balled ready for the fight.

"Girls, you have been friends for as long as you've been in school. Tonight is a night that is supposed to be filled with happiness, joy and anticipation. Why don't we try to let this go until a later date? I think you'll both be happier if you can look back on your prom and remember the good times, don't you?"

"You think I want to remember the time that I wasted on this boyfriend stealing slut? She's too much like her old man, a self absorbed thief!"

"Leave my family out of this, you, you, whore!" Gabby yelled.

Tanya apparently didn't like that term, and her fury took off. She launched herself at Gabby, fists swinging.

"A whore? Who's the whore? Who's pregnant? It ain't me!" Her fist swung wildly.

There was a rush of activity as Mrs. Lerch rushed into the melee to try to break it up. Tanya's groupies didn't want to move to let her through, too entranced in watching the fight.

Ms. Dailey and Mrs. Phelps pushed their way through into the mix. Between the three adults, they were able to get to Tanya who continued to throw punch after punch at the now cowering Gabby.

"You," Mrs. Phelps yelled at the circle of girls, "Out! All of you! Now!"

From just outside the door, I could hear the accusations being thrown around by Tanya, but interestingly, I didn't hear a single word from Gabby.

Suddenly Tanya ran out of the bathroom, with the three adults following; Mrs. Lerch with blood trickling down her cheek.

The rest of the ballroom watched in silence as the four women ran down the hall in ball gowns and heels. Most impressive was Mrs. Phelp's flying tackle, which took out Tanya and a table. Hotel security was immediately descending on them.

"Maybe we should go in and see Gabby," I said to Emily quietly.

"Stevie, I'm not sure that will be—"

Gabby hurried out of the bathroom, took a quick look at us and then headed for a different door. There was something in the look of her eyes that worried me.

"Em, go let Ian know what's going on."

"Where are you going?"

"I'm going to follow her. I'm worried about her."

"You're worried about the girl who has caused you untold amounts of trouble over the years."

"I may not like her much, but right now she needs someone to help her."

I saw Emily shrug as I headed down the corridor, hoping that I could save more than one life tonight.

CHAPTER 22:

BACK WHERE IT STARTED

Heading through a maze of halls, I found myself walking out of the hotel into a parking lot that was bordered by woods. I couldn't help but wonder why every time I felt that I needed to do a good deed, it always began with a trip through the woods.

Walking through the woods in high heels and a ball gown is hard; running after somebody dressed this way is just plain ridiculous. I could hear Gabby running ahead of me, occasionally catching sight of her in the moonlight.

"Gabby!" I yelled, hoping that she would stop and we could talk about things here. Not with my luck. She just kept pushing through.

After what seemed to be an hour, but I knew had been no more than five minutes, I noticed that the trees were thinning. I stepped into the clearing.

I immediately knew where I was. I'd been here several times before over the past few months. Either on my own accord, or brought here by one of the witches in my dreams.

Gabby lay on the ground near the large boulder, weeping. I walked over to her, "Gabby?" I said softly.

"What do you want, Nixon? Come to gloat that you're the goody-goody, and I'm the worthless fool?"

"No," I took a breath, crouched down, and took her hand trusting on my instincts to keep us both safe. Not a gamble I'd take on the average day, but when that's the only choice that you've got, you take it. "No, Gabby, I'm not here to judge or gloat. It just seemed that you really could use a shoulder right about now."

"And after everything that I did to you, you're willing to be that shoulder?"

"Yeah, I am. I know what it's like to feel alone—"

"You don't know anything! You've got that perfect family where everyone gets along. My family's falling apart right now!

And I suppose my cousin's been giving you all of the dirt on the Sosong's, right?"

"Gabby, Ian did tell me about your mom being sick.   But that was only after I'd seen you in the mall. I asked him. Sorry if that makes you uncomfortable."

She let out a deep sigh. "Look, Stevie, thanks for all the concern and stuff, but this doesn't concern you right now." She sat up and leaned against the boulder.

"Gabby, we may not be friends, but you're still a human, and humans are social creatures. We need the support of others to help get us through."

"That's a great thought. Actually, I've got everything that I need right here," she said pulling a small case out of her bra. "When I found out I was pregnant, I went to my folks. My mom about had a conniption; it put her back in the hospital. I realized that I've been nothing but a burden to them. Getting arrested back in March and now this? No, I don't have much to live for. All I've done is cause everyone else grief."

She popped the top to the case, and pulled out several pills.

"Gabby, what are you doing? What are those?"

She turned her head, "What am I doing? I'm ending it all. A few of these and I'll just go to sleep. End of me, end of the problems."

I was at a loss. "Gabby, what about the baby? What did she do to deserve to die before she's ever had a chance to live?"

"I shoulda figured you'd be one of those that believes that. Listen, Stevie, I do appreciate you trying to help me, but the reality is, I'm too far gone."

"No you're not, Gabby." I was grasping at straws here and I knew it. I reached into the bodice of my gown and took out my phone. It was annoying that the guys all had pockets on their tuxes, but the gowns had no place to put things. Originally, I had put my phone in my purse, but digging it out all the time had become too cumbersome, so to Ian's amusement, I'd tucked it into my bra. Now I was so glad that I had.

I fumbled to unlock the screen one handed, but managed to do so and get to my contacts. Scrolling through while keeping my eyes on Gabby, I finally got to Ian's info, and hit send.

"Gabby, listen, we all have problems. But if we work together we can get you through this."

"Work together. Yesterday we couldn't stand each other, now what? We're best buds? Don't think so."

"Do you really think you're the only one who's had problems?" I snapped. "Look around you, Gabby. Everyone has problems of one kind or another. What makes the difference is how we face them. How we choose to take those problems on.

And sometimes, if we're real lucky, we can turns those problems into opportunities."

She laughed, "Opportunities? Yeah, like my circumstances are ever going to give me any opportunities. My mom is suffering from cancer, with the doctors giving her fifty-fifty for survival. My dad's being looked at very carefully by the authorities over some embezzlement that happened at his company. He's already lost his job, so we've already got next to nothing. Now I show up pregnant. Yeah, tell me, where are my opportunities?"

Oh boy, I thought. Guess I stuck my foot in it this time. "Have you considered that after the shock wears off, your folks, will love your baby unconditionally. Maybe she'll be the impetus that will give your mom the strength to hold on and fight through her cancer.

"I'm not saying it's going to be easy, or that it will all turn out roses for you, Gabby, but all we can do is the best that we can." I looked at my phone, it still showed a connection with Ian, so I hoped that he was able to hear what I was saying and was able to get the authorities to track my signal so they would be able to find us. "Have you ever thought about this place?" I asked Gabby.

"What do you mean, this place?'

"This clearing. Why is it here?"

"I can't say that I have. I just know that I've always been drawn here when I wanted to be alone."

"I think it has a familial pull for you," I said.

"What?"

"This ground is sacred for your family, Gabby."

"What did you take, Nixon? You're not making much sense."

"Gabby, you've heard the stories about the headless horseman right?" She nodded, so I went on. "What no one ever told us was that we, you and me, are related to it."

"Are you trying to tell me that you're my long lost cousin or something?"

"No. I'm telling you about a choice, a series of choices actually, that were made right here. Those stories are true. You come from the McCrayn line. Hester and Hubert McCrayn were Icabod Crane's great aunt and uncle. My ancestors had the surname of Brunt, which was a shortened version of Von Brunt. Two hundred years ago, my how-ever-many-greats grandfather killed your equal number of greats uncle. Right here. He threw Icabod's's body over there in the small cave."

"That can't be true. No. How would you know?"

"Because back in your family tree there were those that practiced the art of witch craft."

"Aha!" she shouted. "Now I see what you're doing. You're trying to imply that I've always been cruel to you because I'm a witch. Well, I'm going—"

"Gabby, stick a sock in it. That's not what this is about." She looked at me, now confused. "Two hundred years ago, my ancestor killed yours. Right here, on this very spot. He made a choice, and that choice has had an impact that outlived either of them."

I was edgy now, I needed to pace, but Gabby still had those pills locked in her hand. I tried to just look around to calm myself. "What neither of them knew was that there was a third person that was here as well, the one that created this clearing. When Crane fell and was left, Hester retrieved his body and prepared him for burial. But she also put a curse on my family, one that had persecuted us for generations."

"I'm not part of that curse," Gabby said indignantly.

"No, you're not. However, you are of the blood. This circle is one that has meaning for both of us. It began here, and let's let it end here. I'd like for us to try a fresh start, by being friendly with each other." I extended my hand. "Friends?"

Gabby looked at my outstretched hand tentatively. "I-I guess." The bell in St. Steven's began to chime out the midnight. Our hands met.

Pain shot through my body like I was being electrocuted, while lights flashed in front of my eyes. I tried to scream, but nothing came out. I was falling, spiraling and in agony.

I landed with a crash and my vision began to clear. I could focus only on large objects right now. My head felt as though I had a super-migraine.

Colors started to creep back into my vision. The brown swirl of something close by, the gray of…a rock, maybe? The flashing orange and yellow came with a blast of heat that my mind instantly cataloged as fire.

I recognized the figure in the brown dress. I'd seen her several times before when she intruded into my dreams. I knew that I was back in the same circle, but Gabby wouldn't be here. It would only be the witch who had started this whole mess.

"The tasks of three, I sent to thee, a fourth clue hidden. Ye have tried to prove yeself, but now you're here by my bidding. I cannot lose this game we play, for ye and yours must be forced to pay, and for me to lose is forbidden." She laughed a long loud cackle.

My head was still spinning, but I tried to get to my feet. "What did I fail at?" I demanded. "I was honest with everyone, I proved my loyalty to my friends, and had compassion, for one that I don't always agree with. She was your kin, the one that I helped to save. I've done everything that I could, so no matter what you try to do to me, I'll always have the knowledge that I succeeded, and my honor is strong."

She looked at me, anger flashed as bright as the fire in her eyes. "Your honor, his honor, it matters not. He killed my kin right here upon this very spot. A life he took, must be repaid, his soul must be left to rot. So with this spell, I curse you to—"

A thunderous crash and sparking flames filled the night sky. "Mother, no! Ye must not harm this child. For it's not her doing that got ye riled. For your daughters' sake, we beseech thee please. Let her go, set us free!" She looked over to me, "Remember, Child, remember."

I looked at the witch who had spoken. She was the one from the dream who had told me about the map. To say I was confused would have been an understatement.

The old witch looked at the younger. "Samantha? Why are you here?"

It was the first time that I'd heard any of them speak with out rhyming.

"Mother, yes, it is I. When you cursed that vile man, you used your gift for harm. It affected us as well. Every one of your descendants who had the gift is here now, too. When our earthly bodies die, our souls are trapped here for eternity."

The old witch looked around.

I looked around myself, and was dumbfounded. There had to be at least thirty women standing in the circle, all but the two in front of me, holding hands.

I had to force myself to recall the dream in which Samantha had played a role. Suddenly her words popped into my mind. I whispered "My honor is who I am for the rest of my life. My honor is who I am for the rest of my life." On the third time, I heard the voices of the other women join in. When we finished the simple sentence, I felt a tingling feeling spreading through my body.

The old witch looked at me and then to the younger witch. "It is with sorrow now I see, my rage and temper did this to thee. This one here has proved her worth, let us send her back to earth."

The young witch turned to me, smiled. "Please tell my great-grandson that I'm proud of him. I'm glad he found you." She laid a hand on my head, took the hand of the old witch. In unison they said, "Child, your honor can't be questioned, to great things ye are destined. Remember now the lessons three; honesty, compassion, and loyalty. Every day keep this honor bright and you will have a blessed life. Peace be yours, child."

I felt a warm tingling sensation and my head was spinning again.

"Come on, Stevie, come back to me," Ian's voice rang in my ears while I felt my chest being compressed.

I coughed twice, "Oh, thank God, she's coming around." It was Emily's voice, but it was scratchy. I still couldn't open my eyes.

There was a thrashing sound, "Chrissy and Trevor are waiting for the ambulance. Is she going to be all right, Ian?" Gabby asked.

"I hope so." His voice caught, "She's breathing on her own finally." I felt pressure on my wrist. "Her pulse is coming up, too."

"Gabby, what happened?" Emily asked.

"I honestly don't know. She followed me here, gave me a shoulder to cry on essentially. Then she started talking about some weird curse and how it affected us both. She asked if we could try to be friends. The moment I touched her hand, I got a shock and she dropped. I panicked. Luckily you guys were here within moments."

"It was smart of her to leave her cell on like that," Ian commented.

A hand brushed my hair softly. "Gabby, thanks for helping out here," Ian said. His voice sounded very close to me.

I reached my hand up and grabbed at the one that brushing my hair, "Ian?" I squeaked.

"Yeah, it's me, Stevie. I'm right here."

"Thanks," I said and forced my eyes open so that I could look at him. I reached up and touched his face softly. "Thank you, to all of you. You saved my life."

Chrissy and Trevor led the EMT's to us.

"We saved each other," Gabby said, as she pulled Chrissy and Emily into a small circle around Ian and me. And it was true.

EPILOGUE:

FOUR YEARS LATER

Strolling through the hills just off of Cornell's campus, I walked hand in hand with Ian. "You know," I said as we strolled leisurely along the hiking path. "It's been nearly four years since my brush with the witches of Sleepy Hollow."

"I was thinking about that a bit, too," he said. "We've been together for three of the past five years. I can say that the years that we've been hooked up have been the best for me."

I thought back over those years, our senior year and four years of college. Shortly after graduation from Sleepy Hollow High, Ian and I broke things off for a while. He was having trouble with coming to grips of what his ancestors had done to me. But, we, ended up getting back together after our sophomore year at Cornell, and had been together since. "I'd have to agree. And knowing what I do now, I don't think I'd change the way things happened." I looked up to see him staring down at me. "What?"

"You'd go through that whole curse thing again to get here? Why?"

"You have to look at what that experience brought me. First, and most importantly in my book, I met you. Our paths might have crossed, but would we have become so intimately involved if it wasn't for the curse? I don't know. Then there's your cousin. For many years, we couldn't stand each other. In two weeks I'll be standing as her maid of honor. That never would have happened if it hadn't been for that curse."

"I guess you do have a point," he conceded. "And it's interesting how our little group has expanded to include so many."

I laughed. "Yeah. It's handy that Gabby is marrying your best childhood friend, Jake."

"Sure is. Now I don't have to worry that the best man will be putting the moves on you."

"No, because you know darn well you will be," I laughed.

He pulled me over to one of the overlooks. "There's something that I'd like to ask you."

I looked at him suspiciously. "Okay, what's up?"

"Stevie, we've been through a lot together. But I think we've both discovered that we are stronger together than we are solo. I was wondering," he turned towards me, taking both hands and knelt, "Would you share my life with me as my wife?" He opened a small box that he had cleverly palmed.

I stared open-mouthed. The ring was a simple gold band, topped with a sparkling diamond that wasn't too big but not small. "Yes!" I screamed, and jumped into his lap.

Later that night, we sat in the lounge cuddled together. "Well, my parents are excited," I said.

"That's good. They seemed to like the idea when I talked with them last weekend while we were home."

"When did you talk with them?"

"You were out with Emily and Gabby taking care of last minute things for a wedding. Any idea when you'd like to have a wedding of your own?"

"We'll need to wait a bit. Chrissy's going to graduate from Arizona next May and will be in internships for most of the time until then. Emily's in New York working back stage for Broadway and Gabby's business has a slow season in early summer. Maybe that would work. Do you have any ideas?"

"I'd like early July. Maybe we could do it on the third, you know share your grandparents anniversary. Then we could take advantage of this two week cruise," he handed me a brochure.

"How did you know?"

"I thought it would work after I talked to your mom."

"You're sneaky, Morris. I like that. It'll keep things interesting for the next sixty-plus years."

"I'll keep you on your toes, I promise," he said with that mischievous grin that I loved.

When he leaned over and kissed me, it still made my insides tingle. I love my life.

Keep reading for an excerpt from Christine Chianti's

DESERT DREAMS

Now available from Golden Lark Publishing

www.goldenlarkpublishing.com

Mysterious noises followed her. Jennifer Wolfe kept glancing over her shoulder ready to fend off whatever was chasing her. She was totally unsure what it was, but she knew it was terrible to an unspeakable level. She paused to catch her breath and listened. The darkness that surrounded her gave her no reprieve from her terror. Her ears picked up the labored panting of a large animal combined with the scraping of feet over the loose gravel, the sounds she feared; whatever it was that was chasing her was still coming. There was no escape.

She kept running, her long blonde hair catching on the small branches of the desert brush. Running blind, she hoped that she was heading North; the direction of safety. Without warning she found herself running downhill, and stumbling through the underbrush. Her mind kept fumbling with the one question she really needed to have answered, where was she? Other questions intruded on her already overtaxed mind; who would want to chase her, a freelance photographer, through the desert? And why? She kept pushing forward, her chest burning from the lack of oxygen, her muscles on fire from being pushed beyond their limits and something following her that showed no sign of slowing. With that thought in her mind, her foot caught on what she thought later must have been a tree root and sent her sprawling into the dark.

She landed flat on her stomach, and heard her pursuer behind her slow to a steady march close behind. She rolled onto her back and started wriggling away from the oncoming terror; her eyes desperately trying to peer into the shadows to see her invisible attacker. Suddenly, a face appeared in the darkness, and a scream of terror filled the night.

Darkness flowed in everywhere. Miranda Cassidy was sure that this was some type of dream, but she couldn't find a way to wake up. Then there was that blood -curdling scream that was all too real. She felt her way around but could find no passage to her friend. She fought to overcome the trappings of the suffocating blackness of her imagination, and force herself to wake from the nightmare that she again found herself in. This wasn't real, this wasn't real she kept repeating to herself. Little by little she started to find herself, and the seemingly eternal darkness began to recede. First she was able to feel her head, and then her torso, and finally her limbs came back to life. She forced herself to open her eyes. They balked at the initial attempt, but she kept willing them to open.

There was darkness there too. But as her eyes opened, her other senses began to come back as well; the vanilla scent from the candle that she had burned before bed, the sound of the flowing creek that was in her back yard. Her heart began to settle down into a normal rhythm now that she was more aware of where she was.

Sweating, Miranda sat up slowly and took in her surroundings. She recognized her room bathed in the pale moonlight, so she was in her own home. Reaching over, she turned the switch on the bedside lamp and the light brightened the room. She pulled her knees to her chest and, sitting in bed, began to shake.

This was definitely a bad dream. Curled in her bed, she pulled the blanket around her tightly, and longed for her best friend, Jen. College had really been the only time since first grade that they had been apart. Until now. Jen had been missing for nearly a year and still, no one had any leads on her disappearance

Miranda had stood by her friend at her wedding, even though she didn't care much for the groom. Two years later, she was there again to pick Jen up when the divorce was done. It had taken the better part of a year afterward for Jen to get herself back on a somewhat even keel. That was when she began her around-the-country tour of small towns; photographing the life of the residents. It was while she was in Corona de Tucson, Arizona, almost a full year ago, that she was last heard from. And there had been nothing Miranda could do.

Glancing at the clock on the bedside, she decided it was beyond hope to try to go back to sleep. The alarm would go off in a little more than half an hour anyway telling her it was time to rise and begin the day. She dug her way out of the cocoon of bed covers and shuddered at the early morning temperatures. Even though it was mid June, the temperatures at four A.M. were still a bit chilly.

Heading out of the room, she began her morning ritual. Entering the second door on the right, she turned on the lights and heaters as she prepped her exercise room. It was relatively sparse; only an elliptical machine sat in the corner and reflected in the walls of mirrors. She took her position in the middle of the room and began her yoga routine. For the next sixty minutes, she let the sound of the electric heaters be all she heard as she went through the postures. When she finished, she felt revitalized and ready to face another day.

About Christine Chianti...

Christine is the author of more than twenty titles ranging from short stories to novels. Her latest work, Silver Linings, is the first book in the new Carson Capers series, and will be available in summer 2014.

Christine is a member of Romance Writers of America and is at home in Western New York.

For more on Christine, or her work, please go to:

www.goldenlarkpublishing.com

Connecting with Christine Chianti....

www.christinechianti.com
www.twitter.com/cchianti
www.facebook.com/christinechianti

Other Titles by Christine Chianti:

Short Stories

The Shocking Truth

One Night

New Kid in Town

Novellas

Whole Once More

Novels

Desert Dreams

Fiendish Fall (Sleepy Hollow High: Book 1)

Wicked Winter (Sleepy Hollow High: Book 2)

For more information or to order copies, please visit the publisher
at **www.goldenlarkpublishing.com**